"I'm a far better dancer when I'm allowed to take the lead," Dawson said meaningfully.

"Funny. I feel the same way."

"Do you mean to tell me you always lead?"

"For the most part. You could say it's a habit." Eve's shoulders lifted in a delicate shrug.

He exhaled slowly and shook his head. He felt irritated, frustrated and, God help him, invigorated. "You're something else."

"Thank you."

"I'm not sure I intended that as a compliment."

"No? Well, that's all right." She brought her cheek close to his and he felt her breath caress his ear when she added, "I'm going to take it as one anyway."

Dear Reader

Losing someone dear to us is never easy to accept, but grief can be emotionally crippling if we fail to do so. That's what has happened to my hero in THE TYCOON'S CHRISTMAS PROPOSAL.

Dawson Burke feels responsible for the deaths of his wife and little daughter since he was driving the car at the time of the accident, three years earlier. Since then he has isolated himself from friends and family.

But when he meets personal shopper Eve Hawley, his frozen heart begins to thaw. Life, he soon discovers, has a way of moving on whether we're ready for it or not, and love is a gift to be treasured.

May all your Christmas wishes come true.

Jackie Braun

THE TYCOON'S CHRISTMAS PROPOSAL

BY
JACKIE BRAUN

™MILLS & BOON®
Pure reading pleasure™

Jackie Braun is a three-time RITA® finalist, three-time National Readers' Choice Award finalist, and a past winner of the Rising Star award. She lives in Michigan with her husband and two sons, and can be reached through her website at www.jackiebraun.com

'In 1991 I was sure I was getting an engagement ring for Christmas. So were all of my sisters. The first thing they did when Mark and I walked in the door for dinner was grab my left hand and look. But I didn't get a ring. Mark thought that was too predictable. He proposed to me a few days into the New Year, when I least expected it. I've never regretted saying yes.'

—Jackie Braun,
    THE TYCOON'S CHRISTMAS PROPOSAL

For my late father, Walter Braun.

Thanks for sending down a little inspiration
in the wee hours of the morning, Dad.

I miss you.

CHAPTER ONE

DAWSON BURKE was used to people doing things a certain way. *His* way.

For that reason alone he found the telephone message he'd just retrieved from his voice mail annoying. He flipped his cell phone closed and tapped it against his chin as he stared out the limousine's windows at the fender-to-fender traffic fighting its way into Denver. What did Eve Hawley mean she would be *popping by* his office later today to discuss his gift needs? What was there to discuss?

He'd only met his previous personal shopper on a handful of occasions during the past several years. All other dealings with Carole Deming had been accomplished by telephone, fax, e-mail or proxy. Dawson provided a list of names and the necessary compensation. In return, Carole bought, wrapped and saw to it that his gifts were delivered. Mission accomplished. Everyone happy.

Well, he wasn't happy at the moment.

Eve said she needed to ask him some questions about the intended recipients on his list. Eve said she preferred to meet with her clients face-to-face at least once before setting out to do their shopping. She said it gave her a feel for their tastes and helped her personalize the purchases she made. Eve said...

Dawson scrubbed a hand over his eyes and expelled a ragged breath. This was the third voice mail full of comments and requests that he'd received from the woman. He didn't have time to deal with this bossy stand-in any more than he cared to make time for Christmas. He couldn't help but wonder what had possessed Carole, who was recuperating from knee surgery, to suggest this woman as her replacement.

Maybe he should call Carole and see if she could recommend someone else. Someone who didn't ask unnecessary questions. Someone who simply did his bidding and required no hand-holding.

The limousine pulled to the curb in front of the building that housed the offices of Burke Financial Services. His grandfather, Clive Burke Senior, had started the company, which specialized in managing stock portfolios and corporate pensions. Clive Senior had been gone nearly a dozen years and Dawson's father, Clive Junior, had retired the spring before last. These days, Dawson was the Burke in charge. And he believed in running a tight ship.

His secretary rose from behind her desk just outside his office the moment the elevator doors slid open on the eleventh floor. Her name was Rachel Stern and her surname suited her perfectly. She was an older woman with steel-gray hair, shoulders as wide as a linebacker's and a face that would have made a hardened criminal cross to the opposite side of the street before passing her. In the dozen years Rachel had been in his employ Dawson couldn't recall ever seeing her crack a smile. Stern. That she was, but also efficient and dedicated. He swore sometimes she knew what he wanted before he did.

This morning was no different. She fell into step beside him, prepping him on the day's itinerary even before he had peeled off his leather gloves and shrugged out of his heavy wool overcoat.

"The people from Darien Cooper called. They got held up in traffic and are running about fifteen minutes late. I've put the information packets in the conference room and the PowerPoint presentation is ready to go."

"And my speech for the Denver Economic Club this evening?" he asked.

"Typed, fact-checked and on your desk. The television stations are looking for a preview since their reporters won't be able to get anything back before the late night news. I've taken the liberty of highlighting a couple of points that might make for good sound bites."

"Excellent."

"Oh, and your mother called."

Dawson gritted his teeth. He reminded himself

that the only reason she called him so often was because she loved him and was worried about him. Of
course that did nothing to assuage his guilt. "Does
she want me to call her back?"

"No, she just asked me to remind you to have
your tuxedo dry-cleaned for the ball this weekend.
She's reserved a seat for you at the head table and
won't take no for an answer."

He bit back a sigh. The annual Tallulah Malone
Burke Charity Ball and Auction was the see-and-be-
seen-at event for Denver's social elite. He'd hoped to
send a generous check along with his regrets. But the
ball was celebrating its silver anniversary this year,
and he had little doubt his mother would show up at
his door to personally escort him.

The cause was worthy, raising funds for the area's
less fortunate. At one time Dawson had been happy
to do his part by suiting up like a penguin, shaking
hands and making small talk with Denver's movers
and shakers. But for the past few years he'd made
excuses not to attend the event, which always fell the
second Saturday after Thanksgiving. It was a bad
time of the year for him. The absolute worst, in fact.
He'd been grateful that his mother, who was a stickler
for appearances, had been willing to let him shirk his
responsibilities as a Burke. Apparently his amnesty
had run out.

And she claimed he had inherited his stubborn
streak from his father.

He consulted his watch. "My housekeeper should be in by now. Give her a call. Ingrid will see to it that the tux gets cleaned. And when you get a minute—"

"A cup of coffee and a toasted bagel, light on the cream cheese, with a side of fresh fruit," Rachel finished for him.

"Please."

His efficient secretary could all but read his mind, whereas Eve Hawley apparently was unable to make sense of a simple list of names, even when it included particulars like sex, age and how they were acquainted with Dawson.

"Will there be anything else?" Rachel asked.

"Actually, yes." He retrieved the cell phone from the inside pocket of his suit coat and handed it to her. "Call Miss Hawley back for me. Hers is the third number down. She's the personal shopper Carole recommended. Tell her I'm too busy to see her today and, though it should be completely self-explanatory, see if you can answer the questions she claims to have about the list of names I had you e-mail her last week."

"Very well."

"Thanks." He reached up to massage the back of his neck as he said it, grimacing when pain radiated all the way down his spine. It had been a frequent visitor for the past three years, ever since the car accident that had claimed the lives of his wife and daughter. Tension made the pain worse. This time of the year, when memories and regrets swirled their thickest, it became almost unbearable.

"Is your back bothering you again?" Rachel inquired in a tone devoid of the syrupy concern he so detested. The last thing he wanted was to be the object of pity. Yet he knew that's precisely what he had become in many people's eyes.

Poor Dawson Burke.

"A little."

"I'll call Wanda and see if she can come by for a session between your afternoon meetings today," she said, referring to the masseuse he'd kept on retainer since leaving the hospital after the crash.

That sounded like heaven, but he shook his head. "No time. I ran into Nick Freely on my way out last night. I promised I'd go over some stock options with him."

"I can call him, reschedule," she offered.

"No. I tell you what. Ask Wanda to come by my house this evening. That way I'll be nice and limber for my speech."

When Rachel was gone, he made a mental note to increase the amount on her holiday bonus check. She had it coming.

Eve Hawley had something coming, too, he decided later that evening. And it wasn't monetary compensation.

He was lying on the portable table his masseuse

had set up in the center of his den, only a thin white sheet standing between him and immodesty, when his housekeeper tapped at the door.

"Excuse me, Mr. Burke," she said from the door-way. "There's someone here to see you."

He wasn't expecting company. He had barely an hour before he was due to leave for his speech. As Wanda kneaded his knotted muscles with hands that would have done a lumberjack proud, he asked be-tween gritted teeth, "Who is it?"

"Eve Hawley."

He lifted his face from the donut-shaped rest and gaped at the housekeeper. "She's here now?"

"Yes."

The woman was relentless and obviously inca-pable of doing the job if, even after talking to Rachel, she was still hounding him.

"Tell her I'm indisposed."

"I did, Mr. Burke. But she's insisting on seeing you," Ingrid said.

"Insisting? Well, if she's insisting…" He figured he knew a surefire way to get rid of her. "Send her in."

"Right now?" The housekeeper gaped at him.

"Yes. Right now." If Eve Hawley wanted to see him, Dawson would give her an eyeful.

Ingrid's gaze cut to his bare back and the sheet that rode low across his hips, covering the essentials and then leaving his legs exposed. She was old enough to be his mother. In fact, it was at his mother's suggestion that he'd hired her. Her pursed lips told him exactly how inappropriate she found his suggestion to be. But, like all—or at least the vast majority—of the people in his employ, she minded her own business and did as he asked.

"Very well," she said, withdrawing from the room without further comment.

"Carry on," he told Wanda, before lowering his face back into rest. The masseuse was chopping down his spine in karate fashion when he heard the door open a moment later. The person who entered sucked in a startled breath. Though it was small of him, Dawson grinned at the floor.

"Oh. You're…"

"Busy," came his muffled reply.

Feminine laughter trilled. "Actually, I was going to say naked."

"Not quite." But he frowned at the same floor he'd smiled at a moment earlier. She didn't sound nearly as distressed by that fact as he'd hoped.

"I'm Eve Hawley."

"Yes, I know," he snapped. "Even if my house-keeper hadn't announced your arrival, I would recognize your voice from the many messages you've left on my phone."

"Messages that went unreturned," she had the audacity to point out.

"They were returned. My secretary called you back," he said.

"Ah, yes. Mrs. Stern. If I'd wanted to talk to your secretary, Mr. Burke, I would have dialed her direct. I need to speak to you."

Dawson felt the muscles in his back beginning to tighten again despite Wanda's competent ministrations. "Look, Miss Hawley, surely Carole Deming briefed you on what I'm looking for. This is gift shopping, not rocket science. If you can't do the job—"

"Oh, I can do the job. I just believe in doing it well," she replied in a voice that was stiff with pride. Another place, another time, he might have admired it. He had no patience for it at the moment. "I won't take up much of your time," she promised.

Dawson relented with a sigh, but he didn't raise his head from the padded hole. He was being rude, insufferably so. But then that was the point. The woman already had strained his patience.

"Fine. Shoot."

"You want to discuss this right now?" Her tone was incredulous.

"Right now is all the time I have. My schedule is very tight and will be for the next several days."

"I see." He thought she might object and leave. That had been his goal. But he heard a pair of heels click over the parquet floor. They stopped just outside his limited field of vision.

"I have some concerns," she said, her tone that of a professional who apparently was not the least bit concerned about discussing business with a nearly naked man. Perhaps like the housekeeper, she, too, was old enough to be his mother.

"What are these concerns?"

"Well, in addition to business associates and acquaintances, your gift-giving list includes friends and several family members."

"My parents, sister, her husband and their two children," he said. "I'm well aware of who is on the list, Miss Hawley. After all, I'm the one who made it out." Well, his secretary had done that, but he'd approved the final version.

"I do things a little differently when family members are involved."

Heels clicked on the floor again and Dawson was forced to revise his opinion of her age when a pair of lethal-looking pumps came into view. They were red and made of faux alligator skin. But those weren't the reasons that had Dawson subtracting a few decades from her age. Women of his mother's generation generally didn't have little butterflies tattooed on their ankles.

Curiosity got the better of him. He brought his elbows up and levered partway off the table so that he could see her. Then he sorely wished he hadn't. The rest of Eve Hawley, from the curves that filled out her knit dress to the long dark hair that snaked over her shoulders, was every bit as sexy as her legs and those shoes. Suddenly, the fact that he was nearly naked didn't give Dawson the advantage he'd sought. No.

That had shifted squarely to the black-haired beauty who at the moment was eyeing him with her arms crossed, brows raised and unmistakable amusement glimmering in her eyes.

He sent a glance over his shoulder in the direction of his masseuse. "Wanda, that will be enough for now."

"I don't know, Mr. Burke. You still feel awfully tense to me," she objected.

Out of the corner of his eye, he thought he saw Eve's full lips twitch.

"I'm fine." To Eve he said, "Give me fifteen minutes and we'll go over your concerns."

"Sure."

This time he was positive she was holding back a smile when she sauntered from the room.

Eve waited in a sitting room that was tucked just off the kitchen. The housekeeper had thoughtfully brought her a cup of hot tea. She sipped it now as she stared into the flames of the fire that was flickering cheerfully in the hearth and contemplated her client.

Dawson Burke was a surprise, and not because he'd been clothed in nothing more than a bedsheet at their introduction. He was not the paunchy, middle-aged workaholic who so often relied on her services. God bless those men since they had been helping to pay her bills for nearly a decade, but she hadn't expected Dawson to be quite so young or handsome or—she sipped her tea—physically fit.

As an unattached woman of not quite thirty, there was no way details such as those were going to escape her attention.

Eve was relatively new to the Denver area, and the state of Colorado for that matter. The beauty of her job was that she could do it anywhere. She'd been looking for a fresh start after a particularly nasty breakup the previous spring, and after some Internet research she'd decided that anyplace with a view as pretty and panoramic as the one the Mile High City boasted just might provide it.

So she'd been settling in, building up a client list and sinking down roots. She'd caught a lucky break when she'd met Carole Deming while shopping in a boutique a couple of months back. The two women had hit it off right away. The fact that Carole was fifteen years older and they were technically competitors hadn't stood in the way of their friendship. Indeed, Carole had been kind enough to toss some of her clients Eve's way while she recuperated from surgery.

What was it she'd said about Dawson Burke? "I think you'll find him a challenge."

At the time, Eve had assumed Carole was referring to his gift needs, not his personality. Now she suspected she understood perfectly why the other woman had laughed while saying it. A challenge? Just getting past his pit bull of a secretary had taken an effort, which was why she'd decided to drop by his home unannounced.

Eve didn't mind difficult clients. She'd worked for plenty of them in the past, picky people who gave her cart blanche to buy presents for others or clothing for themselves only to veto her every choice later. But this was different. She simply couldn't do what Dawson wanted her to do without gathering more information, gaining more insight. It wasn't right. As far as Eve was concerned, family members deserved more thought when it came to gifts. She had no qualms about buying for them, but she wouldn't allow the purchases to be impersonal.

She set the tea aside and stood, walking closer to the fire when memories left her chilled. Her mother had died when Eve was eight years old. Suicide, or so it had been rumored. The alternative, an accidental drug overdose, had carried nearly as much stigma, especially since her mother's family blamed her father. Growing up, she'd been shuttled from one relative's house to another's. Her dad had hit the road, ostensibly to try to turn his pipe dream of being a musician into a bona fide profession. More accurately, though, he'd been running from a reality he could not accept.

The last she'd heard, he had a gig at a pub in Myrtle Beach. At nearly sixty, Buck Hawley was no longer waiting for his big break. But he was still running.

He'd missed out on more than two decades of Eve's life, though he always managed to send her a gift to mark another birthday and Christmas. She hated those gifts. They were always impersonal things that Eve knew upon opening he hadn't picked out. For that matter, even the signatures on most of the cards hadn't been his.

While growing up, that had pained her. All these years later it still hurt. She'd needed her father's time, craved his attention as a child. At the very least, she'd wanted to know he thought about her while picking out gifts. So, when clients asked her to buy for their loved ones, she required more than the name and age Dawson had provided on his list.

"Would you care for more tea?"

She turned to find the man in question standing in the doorway. His dark hair was combed back from his forehead, lean cheeks freshly shaved. He was wearing an expertly cut charcoal suit with a white shirt and conservatively patterned tie, yet her heart did the same little somersault it had upon seeing far more of his skin.

"I'm fine." Eve spoke the words for her own benefit as well as his.

He nodded. "Well, not to rush you, but I do have someplace I need to be. I believe you said you wouldn't take much of my time."

"Right." She retrieved her briefcase from the side of the chair. "I do things a little differently than Carole."

"So I gathered," he said dryly.

"For starters, when I shop for close relatives such as those on your list, I need to know something about them." He opened his mouth, but before he could speak Eve added, "Something beyond their sex and age and your price range. For instance, what are their hobbies? Do they have a favorite color? Do they collect something? For the children, are they into video games, sports? Who's their favorite recording artist? And for the record, I don't believe in gift cards, fruit baskets, flower arrangements or the like. Anyone can purchase and send those. They don't take any effort or require any thought. I won't buy gifts like that."

"Maybe I have the wrong person for the job."

Dollar signs flashed in neon green before her eyes. This was a big account, the biggest by far of the ones Carole had fed her. The commission it was likely to bring would go a long way toward fattening up the bank account her cross-country move had depleted. Still, Eve crossed her arms, blinked the dollar signs away and said, "Maybe you do. It's a matter of principle for me."

He studied her a long moment before sighing. "What do you need?"

Eve opened her case and pulled out a folder, which she handed to him. "Given how difficult it's been to reach you, I decided that instead of conducting an interview I would give you this questionnaire. Fill it out at your convenience, but if I could have it back to me by next Monday, that would great."

"Anything else?"

She didn't miss the sarcasm in his tone, but she chose to ignore it. "Actually, there is. While I don't mind flying blind when it comes to buying gifts for business associates and clients, if you have any insights or personal anecdotes about any of the people on your list, I'd welcome them. Feel free to jot down anything that comes to you on the line I've provided next to their names."

"Maybe I should go shopping with you."

Again, she ignored his sarcasm. Smiling sweetly, she replied, "It's kind of you to offer, but that won't be necessary. Unless you really want to. I can always use someone to carry the purchases out to the parking lot."

She wasn't sure why she had just baited him, other than the fact that his arrogance rubbed her the wrong way.

"Excuse me, Mr. Burke?" the housekeeper said from the doorway. "The driver has brought the car around."

"Fine." He turned his attention back to Eve. "I believe we're finished."

"For now," she affirmed and had the satisfaction of watching him scowl.

CHAPTER TWO

DAWSON prided himself on being the sort of man who thought outside the box when finding solutions for problems. It was one of the things that had helped make him a success in business. So, when adversity knocked Friday afternoon, he let opportunity answer the door.

"Your mother is on line one and Eve Hawley is on line two," Rachel informed him.

"I'll take the call from my mother. Tell Miss Hawley I'll call her back." As he said it, he glanced in the direction of his in-box, where the questionnaire she'd given him remained untouched. He had a good idea of the reason behind Eve's call. He also knew why his mother was phoning. The charity ball was Saturday.

"Hello, Mom."

"Dawson, darling. How are you?" she asked.

"Fine."

"So, you always say," she chided. "But I still worry about you."

"There's no need to, really."

But she disagreed. "It's a mother's job."

"I'm an adult, Mom. Thirty-eight last month," he reminded her.

"Your age doesn't matter. Nor, for that matter, does mine." Tallulah was quiet for a moment. Then she said, "I know this is a difficult time of year for you."

"Mom—"

"It's a difficult time of the year for everyone," she went on. "We all miss Sheila and Isabelle."

Hearing the names of his late wife and daughter spoken aloud turned his voice unintentionally crisp, "Don't. Just...don't." He softened the command with "Please."

"Dawson—"

But he held firm, even if he did moderate his tone. "I prefer not to talk about them. I've made my wishes on that very clear."

"What is clear," Tallulah began, "is that you've locked yourself inside a prison of your own making for three very long years. You've always been a fairly rigid individual. But in that time, you've become overly controlling, overly driven. You don't make any time for friends or family, let alone yourself. You spend every waking hour at the office."

"Yes and Burke Financial has thrived as a direct result," he replied. "The last quarter's earnings were the best in the company's history."

"Your father and I don't give a damn about the

business," she snapped. The fact that his mother had used even a mild curse had Dawson blinking in surprise. This was a woman who rarely raised her voice let alone lost her temper. Neither had ever been necessary. She'd always had more effective ways of getting her children to toe the line. She pulled out one of the big guns now. "I hate to say this, Dawson, but I'm very disappointed in you."

He sank back in his chair and closed his eyes. Whether he was eight or thirty-eight, that particular weapon never failed to hit the mark.

His tone was contrite when he said, "I'm sorry you feel that way, Mom. That's certainly not my intent."

"I know." But, of course, she wasn't through. "Have you made plans for the holidays?"

It was a Burke tradition to gather for dinner at his parents' estate on Christmas Eve. In fact, that had been his destination the evening of the crash. Ever since then, he hadn't been able to make it. He expelled a ragged breath. "You know that I have."

"San Tropez again?" she inquired, dismay obvious in her tone.

He'd gone to that tropical paradise the past two years, unable to remain in snowy Denver for the anniversary of that fateful night. This year, however, he'd decided on a different destination. "Actually, I thought I'd try Cabo. I've rented a condo 'til just after the new year."

Like San Tropez, it was warm and sunny with

gorgeous beaches and, most importantly, no one who knew him. People wouldn't ask how he was doing, tilting their head to one side in sympathy as they spoke, or regard him with an overly bright smile that failed to camouflage their pity.

"Alone?" his mother asked.

"Mom—"

But she talked over his objections. "You know, it wouldn't bother me so much that you refuse to spend the holidays with loved ones in Denver if I at least knew you were spending them with someone special."

"I'm fine." He repeated the old saw.

But she threw him a curve. "Are you seeing anyone, Dawson?"

"I've gone out a couple times," he admitted. The dates had been unmitigated disasters, from the stilted conversations at the beginning to the awkward goodnight kisses at the end. Both attempts had left him feeling guilty and angry at fate all over again, but he didn't see any reason to divulge that information to his mother.

She apparently figured it out, though, because she said in a quiet voice, "Oh, son, at some point you need to move on with your life."

"I have," he insisted. He got up each day, didn't he? He went to work. He'd turned the company into an even bigger success than it had been under his father.

As usual, though, his mother cut to the chase. "But you haven't forgiven yourself."

No. He hadn't forgiven himself. He couldn't do that. He closed his eyes, only to see it all happening again. He'd been the one behind the wheel of the car on that snowy Christmas Eve, the one firmly in control of all their destinies until a patch of black ice had changed everything.

Dawson had been the only one to survive the impact with the bridge abutment. He'd walked away with a nasty gash on his forehead and a busted arm. His wife had died instantly, while his daughter had hovered on the brink for several more hours with internal injuries before a surgeon had come out of the operating room to deliver news Dawson still wasn't ready to accept.

"Sorry, Mr. Burke. We did all we could, but we couldn't save her."

How could Dawson forgive himself for that?

His mother's voice snapped him back to the present. "I want you to be happy," she said.

He opened his eyes, rubbed them with his free hand. She didn't get it. No one did. For him, happiness had ceased to be relevant. "Don't worry about me, Mom," he told her for the second time.

But she was saying, "You know, the Harrisons' daughter recently moved back from California."

At that an alarm bell began to sound in his head. He silenced it by saying, "The one who got married a couple of years ago?"

"Yes, but she's divorced now." The alarm sounded

a second time as his mother continued. "I ran into her at the club a couple weeks ago. She still has that same lovely, bubbly personality. She'll be at the ball tomorrow evening. I was thinking of asking her to sit with us. That would give us an even number at our table. And you know how I like an even number."

Dawson straightened in his seat. This was the last thing he needed. The last thing he wanted.

"Mom, I'd really rather you didn't do that."

"She's nice, dear. You'll both have a good time. It doesn't have to lead to anything. In fact, I'm not sure she's ready for a relationship yet herself. Her divorce was final only a few months ago. But at least it will give you both an opportunity to get your feet wet again." Sounding pleased with her plan, she added, "I'll phone her after I hang up."

Good God! His mother setting him up on a date with a newly divorced woman who probably was every bit as unenthusiastic about the matter as he was.

"No!" His gaze caught on the questionnaire Eve had left with him and inspiration struck. Perhaps there was a way he could kill two birds with one stone. His lips curved with a smug smile. "What I mean is, there's no need to do that. As it happens, I already have a date."

Eve was on her way to Boulder, the rear of her Tahoe already laden with the morning's finds in Denver, when her cell trilled. Normally, she didn't like to operate a vehicle and talk on the phone at the same time, but when she saw the number of the person who was calling, she decided to make an exception.

"Hello," she said.

"Hi. It's Dawson Burke."

"Well, this is unexpected."

He sounded confused when he asked, "Didn't my secretary tell you I would be calling?"

"Mrs. Stern? Yes, she did. Which is why I'm in a state of shock. I mean, if I had a dollar for every time your secretary has told me you'd get back with me…" She let her words trail off.

"Very funny," he muttered. "Are you this flippant with all of your clients?"

"Nope. You seem to bring it out in me." But she moderated her tone and added, "Thank you for returning my call."

"You're welcome."

"The reason I phoned you earlier is that I'm on my way down to an art gallery in Boulder to pick up some pieces by a local artist for another client of mine. Buying artwork for someone is like buying clothes. It has to fit the recipient's style."

"Which makes it personal," he said.

"Exactly. So I was wondering if art might be something that would appeal to any of the friends or family members on your list?"

He made a humming noise, then said, "My parents' walls are pretty full at this point and I wouldn't presume to know my sister's taste in art as she's made a hobby out of redecorating her home. My friends...I don't know."

"Oh, well, it was just a thought." Her exit was coming up, so Eve shifted her vehicle to the right lane. "How's the questionnaire coming along?"

She heard him clear his throat. "Actually, I wanted to talk to you about that."

"You haven't filled it out," she guessed.

"Not yet, no."

"Mr. Burke—"

"Dawson, please."

"All right. And you can call me Eve. But I really want that information. I need it, as I explained to you the other night," she said.

"A matter of principle, I believe you said."

"Yes."

"And if I refuse?" he asked. The question sounded almost like a dare.

The dollar signs flashed again, but Eve thought about her father and she remembered her disappointment and heartache. She wasn't willing to pass on those emotions to someone else. Her tone was firm when she replied, "I'd have to ask you to find another personal shopper. So, are you refusing?"

"No, but I have a better idea," he said. "Do you have plans for tomorrow evening?"

"As a matter of fact, I do." Since moving to Denver, Eve had spent nearly every Saturday night alone. But as it happened, she did have something going on. She'd told Carole she would stop by with Chinese food, a bottle of wine and some Christmas movies for the two of them to watch.

"I see." Then he surprised her by asking, "Would it be possible for you to change them?"

Her curiosity was good and stoked. "Why? What do you have in mind?"

"Each year around this time my mother throws a really big to-do. Perhaps you've heard of it? The Tallulah Malone Burke Charity Ball and Auction."

She put on her blinker and maneuvered the Tahoe onto the exit ramp. "No, sorry, but I haven't been in Denver long."

"That's all right. Stick around and you will." There was pride in his tone when he added, "It's been an annual event for the past twenty-five years, drawing in the well-heeled and well-connected to raise money for the area's less fortunate."

"How nice," Eve said and meant it.

"Yes, well, the party is tomorrow night."

Comprehension dawned and something Eve didn't want to admit might be interest danced up her spine. After all, the man wasn't her type at all. Too arrogant. Too domineering. "Are—are you asking me out?"

"Not exactly," he said. "I need an escort for the evening. And you will be compensated."

Indignation blasted along with the horn of the car

behind her, and she realized she'd come to a full stop even though she had the right of way. She sent the other driver a wave of apology and turned into the nearest parking lot.

"Eve?"

She waited until the vehicle was in Park before she let loose. "Maybe I wasn't clear about the nature of the services I provide. I'm a personal *shopper*, not a personal anything else."

She heard Dawson cough. Actually, he sounded as if he might have choked a little, which suited her just fine. He deserved it. Then, he said, "I didn't mean to imply otherwise. Compensation was a poor choice of words. What I meant by it was that many of the people on my gift list will be in attendance. In addition to my parents, sister and her family, a number of business acquaintances and longtime Burke Financial clients attend."

"Oh."

It was on the tip of her tongue to apologize when he added, "I thought seeing them, meeting them, might help you do your job more effectively. You know, live up to those high principles you speak of."

"Are you mocking me?"

"No." He expelled a breath. "For the record, Eve, I admire you for taking a stand. I haven't met many people in business whose principles can hold up under pressure from the bottom line."

He sounded sincere, which went a long way toward soothing her temper. "So, this would be sort of like a business function."

"It would be *exactly* like a business function," he corrected. "But with better food. No rubber chicken or cheap champagne. My mother doesn't believe in doing anything halfway."

As Eve was privy to Dawson's gift budget she decided it was a trait he had inherited.

"It sounds very fancy."

"Black tie required. Do you have something to wear?"

"I think I can find something suitable in my closet," she replied blandly. She sucked in a breath and let it out slowly between her teeth. "Where and what time?"

"Does that mean you'll come?" He sounded surprised and maybe even a little relieved.

She was probably going to hate herself for it later, but she said, "Yes."

"And your other date? I trust that the last-minute change in plans won't cause any...problems."

Eve nearly laughed out loud as it dawned on her that he thought the plans she'd mentioned earlier were with a man. She saw no reason to enlighten him.

So she said, "Don't worry. I can reschedule it. After all, this is work."

CHAPTER THREE

DAWSON cursed and yanked at his bow tie as he stood in front of the vanity mirror. This was his third attempt at tying it and it still had turned out lopsided. He wasn't sure why his hands wouldn't cooperate, any more than he could put a finger on the origin of the nerves fluttering in his stomach.

He hadn't felt keyed up before either of the other dates, disasters that they'd wound up being. And his evening with Eve wasn't a date at all. It was business, he reminded himself, as he finished with his tie, checked his watch and called for his driver to bring the car around.

Business was forgotten, however, the moment Eve opened her apartment door. She was wearing red, her lips and nails painted the same dangerous shade. She'd done something different with her dark hair, pulling it back and up to reveal the slim line of her neck. Diamond studs caught fire on her ear lobes as she tilted her head to one side and regarded him with a smile that he was pretty sure dated back to the original Eve.

"Hello, Dawson."

"You look…" Words failed him. For a moment, he thought his heart might fail him, too. The woman should come with a cardiac arrest warning.

"This works for the occasion, right?" She did a three-hundred-and-sixty-degree turn that made him wish he had a defibrillator handy. "I wouldn't want to stand out."

"You'll stand out, but for all the right reasons," he replied with more honesty than he'd intended.

Her smile bloomed again. "That's quite a compliment. You look pretty good yourself. It's a sin there are so few places for a man to wear a tuxedo nowadays."

"I doubt you'll get many men to agree." He pulled at his collar as he said it. The damned thing seemed to have grown too tight.

Eve laughed. It was a husky sound, entirely too provocative for the mere reason that it wasn't intended to be. "Come on, a tuxedo can't be as uncomfortable as my shoes. My arches are going to hate me by the end of the night."

Dawson allowed his gaze to skim down, which he regretted almost immediately. He'd already known she had a pair of killer legs. Tonight they were accentuated by black pumps that added a good three inches to her already respectable height. His pulse took flight along with the little butterfly tattooed on her ankle. He didn't particularly care for the reaction. Business, he reminded himself.

"Ready to go?" he asked. "While I have no problem arriving fashionably late, my mother is a stickler for punctuality."

"Ah. Right. So, exactly what have you told her about me?"

"Your name."

"A man of few words," she said on a laugh. "Just let me get my coat."

He glanced around while she did so. Her apartment was a loft in a former commercial building that had been converted to residential use. Its exposed ductwork, distressed wood floor and battered brick walls gave it an almost industrial feel. It was small, its total square footage probably not equal to that of his master suite, but Eve certainly had made the most of every inch.

Her taste was as bold and uncompromising as the woman. Vivid colors were splashed against neutrals and a rather eclectic mix of artwork adorned the walls. At the far end of the room, he spied a slim staircase that led to the sleeping loft. A horizontal chrome railing defined the space up top and allowed a tantalizing glimpse of a platform bed beyond. He saw more bold colors there, rich crimsons, plums and golds. For a moment, he allowed himself to wonder what one might interpret from her decorating choices.

"Dawson?"

He turned to find her standing directly behind him. She held a small clutch in her hands and was already wearing her coat, a long wool number that was cinched in at the waist with a belt. Even covered up with not so much as a scrap of red showing, she still exuded far too much sex appeal for his comfort.

He glanced away and cleared his throat. "Nice place you have here."

"Thanks. I like it."

"Excellent location given your job." He made a circular motion with one hand. "Close to shops and all."

"Yes." She smiled. "But work wasn't the only reason I chose it. I like being in the thick of things."

She would. Though he didn't know her very well, he'd already figured out that Eve was the sort of woman who grabbed life with both hands and held on tight, even when the ride got wild.

"Well, we should be going." As he followed her out the door, Dawson wondered why he felt both eager to leave and disappointed that they couldn't stay.

He knew the answer to at least half that question when they arrived at the Wilmington Hotel twenty minutes later. The large ballroom could accommodate seven hundred guests. Only a fraction of that number had arrived, as it was early yet. But his mother gave him a pointed look when she spied him. Dawson sent her a wink and purposely steered Eve in the opposite direction. He needed a little fortification before he faced his family and began fielding their questions. He also needed to clue Eve in on a few pertinent facts.

"How about a glass of wine?" he suggested.

"I suppose that even though this is technically a work function for me a nice glass of Chardonnay wouldn't be out of line," she replied.

"Not at all."

As he ordered their drinks from a bar that had been set up in one corner, Eve said, "I guess you weren't kidding when you said your mother doesn't believe in doing things halfway. I wasn't expecting the party to be quite this large. This room must be set up for at least a few hundred people to dine."

"Seven hundred, actually."

She blinked in surprise. "Is everyone in Denver on the guest list?"

"Sometimes it feels that way," he said. He swept an arm out to the side. "But what you see here are the people with the deepest pockets. My mother's specialty is getting them to reach in, grab a wad of bills and make a donation."

"She sounds like a formidable woman," Eve said.

He merely smiled. She could be, he thought, recalling the previous day's conversation. At times, Tallulah could be downright relentless. The bartender handed them their wine.

"So, is your family here?" Eve inquired, taking a sip. "I'm eager to meet them."

"Some of them are, I believe." He cleared his

throat. "Before I introduce you, though, I need to ask a favor of you. I would prefer that they didn't know what it is you do for a living."

"Ashamed of me?" She tilted her head to one side, sounding more amused than insulted, although he thought he saw something akin to vulnerability flicker briefly in her dark eyes.

"Of course not. It's just that I don't want them to feel…" He groped for the right word.

"Like you brought in a designated hitter because you couldn't be bothered to shop for their gifts yourself?" She smiled sweetly before taking another sip of her wine.

Because his conscience had delivered a swift kick to his nether region, he replied, "You know, you can be annoyingly blunt at times."

Her shoulders lifted in a delicate shrug. "I know. It's a gift."

"It's something," he muttered. "Maybe you should sign up for a Dale Carnegie course."

"I already took one. Passed with flying colors, as a matter of fact. A star pupil." She smiled at him over the rim of her glass. "So, who exactly do they think I am?"

Dawson felt as if he had been dumped back into junior high school when he admitted, "They think you're my date."

"Ah. Your date." She was enjoying his embarrassment. Of that much he was sure. "And how long have we been an item?"

"We're not an item," he groaned.

"First date. Got it." She grinned. "Well, I promise I'll try not to be obvious while I'm plying them with questions to get an idea of their likes and dislikes."

Eve wouldn't be the only one with questions, Dawson thought. Out of the corner of his eye, he spotted his mother. She was homing in on them with the precision of a heat-seeking missile, not even stopping to chat with the people who greeted her along the way. There would be no avoiding her this time.

He put his arm around Eve, leaned close and whispered, "My mother is headed this way."

"Uh-oh. Should I bat my eyelashes at you or something?" she asked.

"This was a bad idea," he mumbled, not quite sure if he felt that way because of her glib reply or because he'd caught a whiff of her perfume. It was sexy, sinful. He ignored the tug of lust it inspired and pasted a smile on his face as his mother reached them.

"Dawson, darling," Tallulah called. "I thought I saw you come in a moment ago."

He kissed her cheek. "Hello, Mom. You look as radiant as ever. Is that a new dress?"

"It is, though I doubt you could give a fig," she replied on a chuckle, letting him know that his attempt at flattery had not sidetracked her in the least. Indeed, speculation lit her eyes even as her lips curved into a smile. "And who might this lovely young woman be?"

Eve knew she was being inspected from head to toe even if Tallulah Burke was smiling and greeting her in as gracious a fashion as she did it.

Dawson performed the introductions, all the while looking uncharacteristically uncomfortable. All of his usual cockiness was gone. Eve liked him all the more for it.

"Mom, this is Eve Hawley. Eve, my mother, Tallulah Burke."

"Eve, it's very nice to meet you." Tallulah shook Eve's hand, covering it with both of hers, which were fine-boned and heavily bejeweled. She didn't let go immediately afterward. No. She held on as she added, "I have to say, I was a little surprised when my son mentioned yesterday that he would be bringing a guest to the party this evening. I wasn't aware he was dating anyone. I guess the mother is the last to know."

Even as she said it, Eve got the feeling that very little got past Dawson's mother. This was no flighty society maven. Her blue eyes were keen with intelligence and, at the moment, a great deal of curiosity.

"Eve and I haven't known one another very long," Dawson hedged.

"Oh?"

"First date," Eve supplied. She didn't quite bat her eyelashes, but came close. Dawson scowled.

"Really? How exactly did you meet?" Tallulah asked, her gaze never wavering from Eve.

"A mutual friend got us together." Since it wasn't exactly a lie, Eve had no problem supplying the information.

Out of the corner of her eye, she saw Dawson nod, apparently pleased with her response. Then, before his mother could probe any further, he added, "It was no one you know, Mom."

Someone called her name then. Tallulah turned and waved. "Well, I need to mingle. You should do the same, Daw. It's expected."

"Right."

She turned to Eve then. "I'll look forward to getting to know you better over dinner."

Oh, I bet you will, Eve thought.

Will I measure up?

The question had her stomach knotting and some of the old insecurities managed to sneak in, despite the fact that her relationship with Dawson wasn't the romantic one his mother had been led to believe.

"I have a feeling that the salmon won't be the only thing grilled here tonight," she murmured once she and Dawson were alone.

"Don't worry. My mother is harmless."

Eve decided to reserve judgment. Admittedly, her first impression of Tallulah had been a positive one. The woman seemed kind, and the very fact that she threw an annual ball to raise funds for charity elevated Eve's opinion of her. But Eve had had enough negative experiences in her past to know better than to trust first impressions.

Pot calling the kettle, she thought, since she did her best to make a stellar first impression. It was important to her.

Thanks to her penchant for sniffing out sales and spending her pennies on quality pieces, Eve knew what to wear. She also had no problem holding her own in social settings. One of the great aunts she'd lived with had been a stickler for etiquette. Eve knew how to sit with her legs crossed demurely at the ankle. She knew how to walk—head up, shoulders back. She knew which fork to use for the various courses served at dinner. And when it came to the art of small talk, she could hold her own with the best of them.

But she was a fraud. An absolute and utter fake underneath all of her props and polish.

She had not been born into money, and, as she'd learned with her last boyfriend, when it came right down to it, for some people it was the pedigree that made all the difference.

Eve notched up her chin, crooked her arm through Dawson's and in her best haughty voice, asked, "Shall we go forth and mingle?"

He heaved a sigh. "I'd rather not, but yes. Just let me do most of the talking."

"Oh, don't worry about me. I'm a regular chameleon," Eve assured him. "No one will ever suspect that I don't belong here."

He sent her a questioning look, which she ignored. Despite those noxious self-doubts, she continued to smile brightly.

Everyone with whom they stopped to chat seemed surprised to see Dawson and, oddly, a little tongue-tied around him. Eve might have thought that was because he was the sort of man who exuded power. Some people found that intimidating. But it was more than his importance. She felt an undercurrent here, something just below the surface of the polite conversations that seemed almost like sympathy. It didn't make sense. Why would anyone feel sorry for Dawson Burke? The man had it made: a high-powered job, wealth, exceptional good looks and a body that appeared to have been chiseled from granite.

Yet for all that, he couldn't manage a real date for an evening. *Hmm...*

As they made their way over to the tables where the items for the silent auction had been set up, Eve said, "I'm curious about something."

"Yes?" he replied absently.

The first item they came to was a gift basket full of aromatherapy bath products. The opening bid was far more than the actual value of the individual components and yet several others had already topped it. Dawson scrawled his name down along with an outrageous amount. She added generous to his list of attributes.

"I'm trying to figure out what's wrong with you," Eve stated bluntly.

He straightened and regarded her from beneath furrowed brows. "Excuse me?"

"Well, you're obviously successful and you're attractive." She gave one bicep a squeeze through the sleeve of his tuxedo jacket. "Your body's definitely all male, even if you do have a penchant for lavender-scented bubble baths."

"It's for charity," came his dry reply.

"Right." She winked because she knew it would annoy him. The man seriously needed to lighten up.

"Charity," he muttered a second time.

"So, why couldn't you get a real date for tonight?"

Dawson looked perplexed by the question. "Aren't you having a good time?"

Surprisingly, she was and so she admitted as much. "All things considered, I'm actually enjoying myself. I'm just, you know…" She motioned with her hand. "Curious."

"Curiosity killed the cat, Eve."

She merely shrugged. "Cats have nine lives. So, why aren't you dating?"

"Who says that I'm not?"

She settled a hand on one hip. "Everyone we've met tonight seems shocked to see you out at a social function." She paused for effect before adding, "Especially in the company of a woman."

"I have a very demanding position as the head of Burke Financial." The excuse was weak and he knew it based on the way his gaze slid away after he said it.

"Okay, got it. Work is the love of your life, so you have no room for a flesh-and-blood woman," Eve deduced, being purposefully blunt.

His gaze snapped back. "I enjoy what I do. There's nothing wrong with that."

"I agree wholeheartedly." She crossed her arms. "I enjoy my job immensely. I'm paid to shop and that's not a bad way to spend the day, in my humble opinion."

Dawson snorted. "Name me a woman on the planet who doesn't like to shop?"

Her eyes narrowed. "Got a pen and piece of paper handy? The list is long, which is why I've remained gainfully employed twelve months of the year since I started doing this. Not everyone who hires me is male or in need of someone to buy their holiday gifts."

His smile was tight when he conceded, "Point taken."

"Actually, my point is that while there's nothing wrong with liking what you do for a living, you also need to enjoy, well, living. That's hard to do when what goes on at the office sucks up nearly every waking hour."

He frowned and said nothing, but for just a moment, when she'd spoken of enjoying life, his expression had turned grim and almost haunted. She'd struck a nerve, of that she was sure. Which nerve, however, remained a mystery.

They moved to the next item up for auction. When Eve saw what it was, she squealed in delight: two tickets to the stage production of *Les Misérables*. Its limited run at the Denver Center for the Performing Arts was scheduled to come to an end just before Christmas. The set of seats being auctioned were prime, a fact that was reflected in the most recent bid. Even so, she snatched up the pencil and jotted down a sum that topped the previous one by twenty-five dollars.

Dawson was rubbing his chin when she straightened. "Your line of work pays very well."

She laughed ruefully. "I'll be eating salad for a month, but I'm dying to see this show. Tickets for seats this good are impossible to get at this point. I've checked. And checked. And checked."

He tapped the paper with the tip of his index finger. "Well, if you really want them, you're going to have to bid higher than that."

"You think?"

"I know. The evening's young yet and the people with the fattest wallets tend to arrive fashionably late to these things."

"Great," she muttered.

"You can always buy the soundtrack."

"I have the soundtrack." She listened to it so often she could sing every song from memory. Sucking a breath between her teeth, she leaned over to erase her first bid. Then she raised the previous amount by fifty dollars. Afterward, she sent him a weak smile.

"I like salad and I've been meaning to lose a few pounds anyway."

His gaze detoured south and his brows rose right along with her pulse rate. Though he said nothing, his eyes communicated something quite clearly. She knew that look. It was all male and interested. Her heart thudded in response, which struck her as outrageous since she wasn't even sure she liked Dawson Burke. Of course, like and lust weren't mutually exclusive.

Then he shrugged and his expression once again turned aloof and arrogant, leaving her libido feeling duped.

They moved on. Standing before the next auction item was a couple Dawson apparently knew well.

"Hey, look who's here," the man said, smiling as he reached out to clasp Dawson's hand.

"Hi, Tony. Christine," he added, leaning over to buss the woman's cheek. "It's been awhile."

"That's because you haven't returned any of our phone calls," Tony reprimanded lightly.

Apparently he made a habit of that, Eve thought.

"We've been worried about you," Christine added.

Dawson cleared his throat as he sent a fleeting glance in Eve's direction. "There's no need to worry about me."

The couple followed the direction of his gaze, spied Eve and attached a far different meaning to his glance.

"So we see. We're glad for you, Daw," Christine said. "Really, glad."

"Yeah," her husband added. "It's about damned time you returned to the land of the living."

Because he hadn't actually introduced her, Eve did the honors herself. She recognized their names from Dawson's gift list, so she discreetly sized them up during the brief conversation, trying to concentrate on the kind of item that might suit their tastes, rather than their curious comments that Dawson had already made clear related to something that was none of her business.

"Well, we probably should make our way to the head table," he said, winding up the conversation just after Christine mentioned running into the parents of someone named Sheila at the theater recently. "It was nice seeing you both again."

"Yes. We'll be having our annual party weekend after next. The invitations go out on Monday. Do you think you might make it this year?" Tony asked. "And, of course, Eve is welcome to come, too." He sent a smile in her direction.

Uh-oh.

But she was saved from having to answer. Dawson was shaking his head. "Sorry. Other plans."

"Oh." Tony shrugged, though he was clearly disappointed. "Maybe we can get together for dinner one night between Christmas and New Year's. Christine and I have been meaning to try out that new steak house."

"Sorry," Dawson said again. "I'll be in Cabo from Christmas Eve 'til the first of the year."

"Cabo?" Tony glanced at Eve and then back at Dawson. "I guess I thought that maybe this year..." His words trailed off awkwardly.

"We should head to our table, too," Christine said, taking her husband's arm and sending a tight smile in Dawson's direction. "It was nice meeting you, Eve. Hopefully we'll see you again."

Though it was the other couple who moved away, Eve was left with the distinct impression that Dawson was the one who had gone somewhere else.

CHAPTER FOUR

"DAWSON?"

He blinked twice and seemed to snap out of whatever fog he'd been in. "Yes?"

"You mentioned something about taking our seats," Eve reminded him.

"Right." He put a hand on the small of her back, guiding her away. He didn't sound irritated, but weary, when he said, "I've done just about all of the mingling I can stand."

The head table was at the front of the ballroom just to the right of a raised stage, presumably for easy access to the podium and microphone. The table was round and had place settings for eight. A woman with two young boys was already seated there. The boys were slouched down in their chairs, looking sullen and subdued, but their expressions brightened considerably when they spied Dawson.

"Uncle Dawson!" they squealed in unison.

"You're here!" the older one said.

To which the younger one added, "Mom bet Dad that you'd find an excuse not to show up, even though you promised Nana you'd come this year."

"You're not supposed to tell him that," the other boy said, rolling his eyes in disgust.

"Why not? It's true."

"You're so lame."

"Boys, no name calling," their mother warned. Then she said, "Hello, Daw."

"Hello." But he returned his attention to his nephews. "Nice suits." Like all of the men in the room, the boys were outfitted in black tuxedos. The only difference was that their ties were askew and their white shirts were looking wrinkled and coming untucked. Eve found them adorable.

"Mom made us wear them," the younger one grumbled, pulling at his collar.

"I know how you feel," Dawson said on a chuckle. He put his hand behind Eve's back and drew her forward. "I'd like you to meet my guest, Eve Hawley. Eve, these are my nephews, Brian and Colton. Brian is eight and Colton is ten."

"I'm nine, Uncle Dawson," Brian corrected.

"And I turned eleven over the summer. Remember? You couldn't make it for dinner, but you sent me that chemistry set." The way Colton's mouth twisted on the words told Eve exactly what the boy thought of the gift. She'd bet someone else—Carole, perhaps?—had purchased it.

"Ah. Right. Nine and eleven," he repeated on a nod, looking slightly embarrassed. Was that because he'd forgotten their ages or because the gift had obviously been "lame," to use the boy's vernacular.

"Well, it's nice to meet you both," Eve said and she meant it. She was determined that by the end of the evening she would have a good idea of the kind of gift they would cherish from an uncle they clearly adored.

"Are you going to introduce us, Daw?" the woman asked. Dawson's sister shared his dark coloring, with the added bonus of having their mother's startlingly blue eyes. She was a striking woman—a striking woman who at the moment also looked openly curious.

"I'm not sure I should," he said.

"Fine, then I'll do it myself." She stood and smiled at Eve. "I'm Lisa Granderson, this ill-mannered buffoon's younger sister."

"Hello, Lisa. It's nice to meet you." That seemed to be Eve's stock phrase this evening…and the evening was young yet.

The other woman studied her a moment. Eve felt herself brace. But all Lisa said was, "I love your dress, by the way. That color looks incredible on you." Her gaze slid to Dawson. "Don't you agree?"

"Incredible," he said stiffly.

"Thank you."

"Why don't you sit next to me?" Lisa invited. "We can talk fashion and you can tell me how you were able to drag my reclusive brother out of his cave for the evening."

"Sorry. Mom has the seating arranged," Dawson said before Eve could respond. Picking up a small place card, he told his sister, "Eve is next to Colton. It looks like Mom's put you next to David." He glanced around then. "Speaking of your husband, where is he?"

"He and Dad are out by the coat check." Lisa rolled her eyes as she added, "They're listening to the last period of the hockey game on David's iPod."

"The Avalanche are playing the Red Wings," Colton supplied.

Dawson snorted as he shook his head. "Does Mom know what they're doing?"

"What do you think?" Lisa said.

"I think if she catches them, there's going to be hell to pay." Dawson chuckled after saying it. The sound was a bit rusty at first, but it wound up rich and inviting.

His reaction surprised Eve. She hadn't been aware the man knew how to smile let alone give in to mirth. Apparently, she wasn't the only one in shock. All eyes at the table had turned to him. But it was his sister's expression that caught Eve's notice. Lisa looked wistful and…hopeful?

"God, I've missed you," she said, her eyes turning bright. "I'm so glad you came tonight, Daw."

He unbuttoned his jacket and tucked his hands into the front pockets of his trousers. Though his shrug was intended to be casual, Eve saw the discomfort he tried to hide. "You know Mom. She wouldn't take no for an answer since this is the silver anniversary of the party."

"Well, whatever the reason, I'm glad you're here. And it's good to hear you laughing again," Lisa said.

Dawson glanced Eve's way, but then his attention was diverted by an older man, who slapped his back before pulling him in for a bear hug.

"Dawson! You made it."

The man was the same height as Dawson, although his build was a little thicker and less muscled. He was handsome, distinguished in the way men get from the same crow's feet and silver hair that women paid big money to diminish and conceal. Eve would have figured out his identity even if Dawson hadn't said, "Hello, Dad. How are you?"

"Better now that you're here."

Was Dawson the black sheep of the family? The prodigal son returning? Eve couldn't help but wonder given all of the comments.

"So, what's the score of the hockey game?" Dawson asked.

The older man shook his head in disgust. "The Avalanche are down by two. They should have traded that goalie when they had the chance."

"Actually, they're down by three now," inserted a younger man Eve assumed was Lisa's husband, David. "Detroit just scored during the power play."

At this, Lisa stood. "That's it." She settled one hand on her hip and held out the other. "Give me the iPod before Mom gets to the table and pitches a fit." She nodded in Eve's direction then. "And before Dawson's date gets the impression that his family is completely backward."

"Dawson has a date?" David asked as he handed over the iPod, earpiece and all.

"Yes, he does." This comment came from Tallulah as she joined them at the table. Eve felt her stomach knot. And that was before the woman smiled brightly and said, "Why don't you introduce Eve to everyone, Daw, and then we can all sit down and start getting better acquainted."

After he made the introductions, Tallulah said, "Eve, dear, why don't you tell us a little bit about yourself?"

She smiled easily even as she straightened in her seat. "What exactly would you like to know?"

"Anything you wish to share. This isn't an inquisition, dear." Tallulah laughed, intending to put her at ease.

"No, that comes later," David inserted sotto voce. Lisa slapped his arm and the boys giggled. Dawson's expression softened.

"Why don't you start with where you're from?" Tallulah said. "I detect an accent of sorts in your speech."

"Actually, I was thinking the same thing about all of you," Eve replied without missing a beat. Then she added, "I'm from Maine originally. I was born in Bangor. I guess to folks here it probably sounds as if I flatten my vowels."

"Maine? You're a long way from home," Tallulah said.

"Do you have family here?" Lisa asked.

"No. No family here." At least she didn't think so. But her father tended to get around. In college she'd gone into a Daytona Beach bar while on spring break only to discover her dad was the opening act for the band.

"What brought you to Denver?" Dawson asked.

"I came here for the view."

"That's an interesting reason to pull up stakes and move across the country," he said.

"I was ready for a change of scenery."

"What about a job?" his father asked. "Did you have something lined up here?"

"Not exactly, but I had no problem finding employment once I arrived."

"What line of work are you in?" his mother asked.

Eve felt Dawson's foot nudge hers beneath the table. He needn't have worried. She'd told him she wouldn't lie and once again she didn't have to. "I specialize in sales," she said.

"Well, if you ever need any investment advice, go see Daw. He's got the Midas touch when it comes to picking stocks." Tallulah beamed with pride.

Eve eyed him speculatively. "Really? The Midas

touch." She wondered what other things could be said about the man's touch. "I'll keep that in mind."

For the next several minutes, while his family subtly grilled Eve, she returned the favor. And not just for work purposes. They were an interesting and likeable bunch. Despite their obvious curiosity about her, they were warm and inviting. They were not in the least what she'd expected. Given Dawson's wealth, she'd figured his family for upper crust, emphasis on crust. She'd been prepared for them to be distant or act superior. Drew's family had been outright judgmental of those who came from less affluent families.

The Burkes were anything but.

Dawson was turning out to be a surprise, too. There was far more to the man than first met the eye, which was saying a lot given how little he'd been wearing at their first meeting.

At first she'd pegged him as a workaholic who was too busy to buy gifts even for his family. Then she'd thought that maybe he was a self-absorbed CEO who was indifferent to everyone around him and estranged from his loved ones.

But his family obviously adored him, and though he wasn't overly demonstrative, it appeared the feeling was mutual.

"Eve?" He leaned over to say it.

"Hmm, yes?" When she turned, their cheeks brushed.

"Come to any conclusions?" he whispered.

"No," she admitted. Then blinked. "Oh, do you mean about gifts?"

He frowned. "Of course I mean gifts. What were you referring to?"

She shook her head and worked up a smile. "Nothing." Because he was still frowning, she added, "I might not have actual gifts in mind, but I'm definitely getting a good idea of personalities."

With that she reminded herself that her reason for being there this evening wasn't to probe into Dawson's motivations for hiring her or to delve into his past. She was at the charity ball to find out more about the people on his list, in particular the members of his family. So, after Tallulah took the stage to welcome everyone and ask them to be seated for dinner, Eve took her assigned seat next to Colton. In between making polite conversation with the adults, she began to subtly pump both boys for information about their hobbies and extracurricular activities. By the time the salad plates were being removed to make way from the main course, she was pleased to have already come up with some excellent leads.

While the waitstaff brought dishes laden with pork tenderloin, grilled salmon, chicken marsala and an assortment of steamed vegetables, rice and boiled red-skinned potatoes to each table, Dawson pretended to follow his father's lament over the Fed's decision to raise the interest rate a quarter point. In truth he was listening to Eve and his nephews discuss videogame strategies.

She was talking them through level six of what was apparently one of the hottest games among prepubescent boys if his nephews' reactions were any indication. Brian and Colton were absolutely enthralled.

Dawson was, too. But in his case it had less to do with her tips on how to defeat a dragon and secure extra lives than the effect her laughter was having on him. Though she had a job to do, she obviously liked kids.

Eve glanced up and caught him staring. "What?" she mouthed.

He shook his head and mouthed back, "Nothing."

How could he tell her that he hadn't expected someone who looked as glamorous as she did to be such a natural with kids?

She'd probably be insulted, though he considered it a compliment. A lot of women he knew weren't overly fond of kids. Even his late wife hadn't been comfortable around children. Oh, she'd adored their daughter, and Dawson had been close to persuading Sheila to try for a second just before the accident. But she hadn't been the hands-on sort, preferring to relinquish what she called "the minutia of child-rearing" to a nanny. That had been a source of friction in their marriage, since their opinions of what constituted minutia differed greatly.

Like Sheila, Dawson had grown up with every

advantage and luxury at his disposal thanks to his parents' wealth. But while his mother had been practical enough to delegate certain responsibilities such as cooking, cleaning and, at times, carpooling to the hired help, she'd been integrally involved in all aspects of her children's lives.

That hadn't changed even though they'd grown up and moved out. Across the table, he heard his sister and mother arguing over the current length of hemlines.

"There's nothing wrong with showing a little more leg," Lisa said.

"If you're young and have long, slim legs like yours or Eve's, no," Tallulah agreed. In the dim light, he thought Eve flushed. "But women my age or who have put on a few too many pounds, shouldn't show so much skin. It's not attractive."

"You could show a little more skin for my taste," Clive said, sending his wife of forty years a bold wink.

Tallulah wagged a finger in his direction. "Stop flirting with me in front of the children."

Laughter erupted. Eve joined in. Dawson did as well. Afterward, his chest ached. He'd missed this, he realized. The good-natured bickering, the teasing, the laughter.

He'd always been the most serious of the Burke bunch, a trait his father claimed had skipped a generation and come directly to Dawson from Clive Senior.

Grandfather had been an imposing man, downright rigid in some ways. Dawson's father had called the older man Sir until the day he died. Perhaps that was why he insisted that his own children call him Dad and his grandkids call him the more informal Grandpa or Gramps. So, the comparison to Clive Senior wasn't exactly a compliment. These days, Dawson supposed, it was more apt than ever.

He glanced around the table at the smiling faces of his family and then finally at Eve. She was smiling, too. Looking radiant, lovely and so...alive.

For the first time since the accident, Dawson's regret was not that he hadn't died with his wife and daughter, but that he'd forgotten how to live.

CHAPTER FIVE

WHEN the meal was finished and the servers began clearing away the dishes, Tallulah once again took to the stage. This time, as she stood at the podium, she reminded her guests why they had come.

"Thanks to your past generosity, a lot of lives have been changed for the better. I know I can count on that generosity again tonight. The silent auction will close in another hour. If you aren't lucky enough to take home one of the incredible items supplied by our various sponsors, you're welcome to make a donation.

"In the meantime, please enjoy yourselves. We have a wonderful DJ, Dan Williams, on hand. So, let the dancing begin."

After Tallulah exited the stage to applause, the music began to play. The DJ kicked off with a slow number in deference to the fact that people had just finished their meals. Dawson leaned back in his seat, biding his time. Another hour or so and he could leave, his duty to his family fulfilled as well as his duty to Eve. Surely by then she would have enough information to do her job.

She had turned sideways in her seat so that she could see the stage. Now that the music was playing, one of her feet had begun to tap. The polite thing to do would be to ask her to dance. His mother was giving him pointed looks in that regard. But he didn't. Dancing required entirely too much physical contact for his comfort.

He should have known Eve wasn't the sort of woman who would wait to be asked. Bold, he thought again, when her gaze locked with his and she smiled.

"Do you dance?"

He made a dismissive sound. "It's been awhile."

And it had. The last time he had been on a dance floor, he'd been here. With his wife. While their daughter slumbered safely at home under the watchful eye of a sitter. The realization caused him to frown.

"No need to look so distressed," Eve assured him, misinterpreting his pained expression. "I hear it's like riding a bike. You never forget how."

"I'm not—"

But she was already laying her napkin aside and rising to her feet.

"Come on. It will be fun."

Fun? He doubted that. But his family was watching, his mother nodding in approval, his sister's eyes growing misty again.

"Very well."

He and Eve were the first couple on the dance floor. The only couple, in fact. They might as well have had a spotlight shining down on them. The music was too loud to hear, but Dawson imagined the murmurs coming from the crowd as he took Eve in his arms.

In addition to feeling conspicuous, he felt wooden and awkward as the past and the present intertwined, making way for comparisons that he didn't particularly like. Sheila had been petite, her build small and delicate. Eve was tall for a woman and her heels made them nearly the same height. He rested one palm just above her hip and grasped her hand, determined to keep a respectable distance between his body and her dangerous curves.

As soon as they began to move to the music, however, that space began to evaporate. Thighs mingled. Their hips bumped. Sheila had been pliant in Dawson's arms, going in whatever direction he chose. Not Eve. It was clear almost immediately that he was not the one in control.

A tendril of her hair tickled his nose when he turned his head to whisper, "You're leading."

"Yes, I am." She said it without a hint of apology. Then she asked sweetly, "Do you have a problem with taking instruction?"

"A problem? No. Not really. I simply prefer to give it." He attempted to back away, but the scent of her perfume followed right along with the rest of her. Before he knew it, she was close enough to his body that he swore he could feel the vibration when she made a tsking sound.

"And here I thought you were original, Dawson. But that's such a typical male response. It's a good thing I'm wearing high heels or I'd be drowning in testosterone."

"Funny."

Eve executed a turn that Dawson wasn't prepared for and he stepped on her toes. She grimaced.

"I should apologize for that, but I find myself wanting to say it serves you right. I'm a far better dancer when I'm allowed to take the lead," he said meaningfully.

"Funny. I feel the same way."

That had him frowning. "Do you mean to tell me you always lead?"

"For the most part. You could say it's a habit." Her shoulders lifted in a delicate shrug.

"Just what kind of men do you date that leading while dancing has become a habit for you?" he asked.

"The kind who are secure in their manhood," she replied. She leaned back as she said it. Amusement glittered in her dark eyes. She knew she had him. There wasn't much he could say in response to that without impugning himself.

Dawson exhaled slowly and shook his head. He felt irritated, frustrated and, God help him, invigorated. "You're something else."

"Thank you."

"I'm not sure I intended that as a compliment."

"No? Well, that's all right." She brought her cheek close to his and he felt her breath caress his ear when she added, "I'm going to take it as one anyway. Lemons from lemonade, that's my motto."

Dawson gave in and let Eve lead for the rest of the song. It was either that or he was going to continue to knock knees with her and step on her toes. He preferred not to make an even greater spectacle of himself, even if it meant handing over control.

Thankfully, by the time the song ended, they weren't alone on the floor any longer. Several other couples had joined them, including his parents. Clive and Tallulah were smiling at him. He could only imagine what conclusions they were reaching, especially when, as another slow song started, Eve was still in his arms.

"Care to do this again?" she asked. She sweetened the deal by adding, "I'll be good and let you lead."

Because he felt just a little too tempted, he shook his head and released her. "Maybe another time."

They stayed at the ball for another hour and a half, which was long enough to hear the results of the silent auction. Eve didn't win the theater tickets, but then Dawson had known that her bid, generous though it was given her means, ultimately wouldn't be enough. Indeed, the winner had outbid her by nearly five hundred dollars. This was for charity, after all.

"Oh, well," she said when the winner was an-announced. "I've got the musical's soundtrack."

"Maybe you can listen to it while you dine on lobster," he said, referring to her earlier mention of having to eat salads if she won.

But she was shaking her head. "Lobster? I'm from Maine. Once you've had it there, where it's caught in the morning and on your plate that after-noon, you're pretty well spoiled. I'll have a steak. A nice, juicy T-bone cooked so rare that it melts in your mouth."

His own mouth began watering when she made a little humming noise. To his mortification, her benign talk of red meat was whetting far different appetites. He glanced at his watch. It was just after ten. He was relieved that the evening was almost over, and not just because of his unexpected attraction to Eve.

Even though the point of bringing her had been to introduce her to his family and some of the other people on his Christmas list, he wasn't sure he appre-ciated the way she'd been received. Everyone liked her. No surprise there. She was a likeable woman, not in spite of her outspoken nature, but in some ways be-cause of it. But it was more than that. He saw the speculation in their gazes and read between the lines in their comments. He knew what they were thinking: he had finally moved on with his life.

Nothing illustrated this more than his mother's question while he and Eve were saying their goodbyes.

"Will you be coming to dinner tomorrow afternoon?" Tallulah inquired.

Sunday dinner with his parents was a tradition, or at least it had been until the accident. He, Sheila and Isabelle had rarely missed it. In the intervening years, however, he could count on one hand the number of times he'd shown up.

So he shrugged. "I don't know, Mom. I have a lot I want to wrap up."

Tallulah nodded, not quite able to hide her disappointment. "Before you leave for Cabo."

He swallowed. "Yeah."

She forced a smile to her lips and sidled closer. "Well, if you change your mind, I hope you'll bring Eve. She's delightful, Daw."

He cleared his throat. "It's not what you think, Mom. Eve and I aren't...serious."

"Maybe you should be."

Dawson thought about his mother's remark during the ride home. Eve was seated next to him on the limousine's plush leather seat. She was wrapped up in her long wool coat. Even so, the scent of her perfume kept drifting to him, just as it had on the dance floor. It was sexy, dangerous. It slipped over and around him and cinched like a lasso. He found it a small consolation that the woman was completely unaware that his insides were being trussed up like a rodeo steer. She was talking business.

She had pulled a personal digital assistant from her clutch and was entering in some notes as she talked. "I couldn't help but notice your mother's jewelry. She's obviously very fond of gemstones."

He snorted at the understatement. As far as he knew, it was his mother's one weakness. "If it sparkles, she's got to have it."

"There's a boutique in town that carries one-of-a-kind pieces from a Venetian artisan. His work is quite remarkable and of the highest quality. I was in the shop last month to purchase something for another client and remember seeing some lovely rings. I'll pay him a visit first thing Monday and let you know what I find."

She shifted in her seat, undoing the top button of her coat and loosening the silk scarf beneath it. Her perfume wafted to him and once again had him thinking about sex—the act itself and how long it had been since he'd engaged in it. He'd work out when he got home. Thirty minutes with the free weights should do it. Followed by a cold shower, he amended when she began to suck on the end of the PDA's stylus.

"Okay," he managed.

"As for the boys, that's easy. They're salivating for that new gaming system."

"Every kid in the country is," he said on a snort. "It's the hot toy this year."

"I know. When we were in the ladies' room, your sister admitted to me that she hasn't been able to find one anywhere. All the stores she's tried have been sold out and they can't guarantee they'll get another shipment in before Christmas. She was thinking of going online and paying a private seller whatever price it takes. I talked her out of it. I told her I was pretty sure you'd already gotten them one. You should have seen the look of relief on her face."

"Great. How are you going to track one down if she's been unsuccessful?" he asked.

She sent him a wink. "I have my ways."

He meant it when he said, "If you pull this off, they'll be in heaven."

"Yes, and you'll be their hero, Uncle Dawson." She sent him a grin.

He glanced away, uncomfortable to be cast in that role. "I'll just be happy to redeem myself for the chemistry set fiasco."

"Did you pick out that gift yourself?" she asked.

"No. Actually, Mrs. Stern was the one who bought and sent it."

"Why am I not surprised?" she muttered.

"What?"

"Nothing." She waved a hand and then went on. "During dessert I heard Lisa say something to your mother about a Misty Stark dress she bought recently. I was thinking that a handbag from the designer's new collection might be a winner."

"She likes handbags," he said. "She probably needs a walk-in closet just to accommodate the ones she has now."

Eve smiled at him. "I knew I liked her."

He folded his arms. "What is it with women and purses? How many do you need?"

"One to go with every outfit and to suit every mood. In other words, you can never have too many. Handbags are like shoes that way."

"God, you sound like my wife." The words were out and, judging from Eve's stunned expression, he wasn't going to be able to pretend he hadn't said them.

Nor was he going to be able to change the subject, he realized, when she said, "Do you mean as in ex-wife?"

"No. As in late wife. She…she and my daughter died in a car accident." He swallowed the bitter memories and absently rubbed a hand over the raised scar that was partially hidden in his hairline.

"My God, Dawson. I had no idea. I'm so sorry."

She rested a hand on his forearm and gave it a squeeze. He nodded stiffly to accept her condolences and then moved slightly, forcing her hand to drop.

"When did this happen?"

"Three years ago." He cleared his throat. "Look, no offense, but this isn't something I care to talk about. Mind if we change the subject?"

She nodded. "Of course."

Even so, the remainder of the drive to her apartment was accomplished in silence.

* * *

Well, Eve thought, some things about the man—not to mention the interesting reactions he'd received all evening—finally made sense. But far from alleviating her curiosity, this new bit of information stoked it more.

Three years was a long time. But not when tragedy was involved. Tragedies changed people. Eve knew that firsthand. As young as she'd been at the time of her mother's death, it had shaped her life. In a way, she'd lost both of her parents—her mother to an overdose, her father to the road. Her mother's death had certainly changed her father.

How had tragedy changed Dawson? And she had little doubt it had, especially after meeting his family. What had he been like before the accident?

When they arrived at her apartment building, he walked her to her door. She expected that. He was a gentleman, and having met his mother, Eve knew good manners had been drilled into him.

"Tonight was very productive," she said.

He was standing on the opposite side of the small elevator, studying her. "That was the purpose."

"Yes. But I had a nice time anyway. You have a great family," she told him.

His head jerked down in what resembled a nod. He said nothing.

They arrived at her door. Eve wasn't sure what prompted the invitation, but she asked, "Would you like to come in for a drink?"

His jaw clenched. "It's getting late."

Because she felt foolish, she teased, "Worried that you'll turn into a pumpkin?"

He snorted. "Worried that my driver might."

"Jonas, right?" She'd forgotten about him.

"Right."

She pulled the keys from her small clutch. "Well, I'd offer to invite Jonas in for a nightcap as well, but I wouldn't want to give you the wrong impression about me."

Dawson laughed at that remark. The sound was rusty but pleasing. "Since the first moment I met you, Eve, I've formed all sorts of impressions. I don't think I've figured you out yet." He sobered, leaned against the doorjamb and studied her in the hallway's dim lighting. "You have a lot of layers."

"If you compare me to an onion you'll ruin what is otherwise a fairly interesting compliment."

His eyes narrowed. "Why do I get the feeling you like to keep me guessing?"

She batted her lashes. "Maybe because mystery is half of my allure."

He straightened and she thought he might turn to leave. In fact, she swore he started to, but then he was closing the space between them.

In that brief moment as his mouth hovered just above hers, Dawson whispered, "Don't sell yourself short."

As kisses went this one shouldn't have rocked

Eve's world. It was brief, close-mouthed and nearly perfunctory. Yet her knees felt weak afterward.

She credited Dawson's expression for that. She'd seen the man nearly naked, but at the moment he was far more exposed. Emotions played over his face in rapid succession, so many that she could barely keep track of them. But a couple stood out. He definitely looked angry and he most certainly was turned on.

We're even, she thought, as he stalked down the hall and she closed the door.

CHAPTER SIX

"You might have mentioned something to me about Dawson's having lost his wife and child," Eve said.

She was at Carole's comfortable home just outside Denver, making good on the movie, wine and Chinese food night that she'd previously had to cancel. Carole's leg was propped up on a pillow on the couch and an old Cary Grant movie was playing on the television, though neither one of them was watching it.

Between bites of sweet and sour pork Carole admitted, "I thought about it. In fact, I nearly did when you said he wanted you to come to the charity ball. But I wanted you to form your own impression of the man without being prejudiced by his tragic history."

"Why?"

Carole shook her head. "We'll get to that in a minute. First, I want to hear what you think about him, especially after spending an entire evening in his company."

"You make it sound like it was a date," Eve said dryly. "It was work."

Her gaze slid away. Well, it *had* been mostly work. The big exception of course was the kiss he'd given her at her apartment door. While it had ended well before turning into anything remotely passionate, it had been on her mind ever since. Were Dawson a different sort of man, Eve might have thought that was his intent.

Keep her guessing…

Keep her wanting…

As it was, she doubted he'd meant to lock lips with her in the first place. Afterward, he'd barely managed to bid her a curt good-night before stalking away.

"Are you going to tell me you didn't enjoy yourself?" Carole asked.

"No. I enjoyed myself." It was easier to concentrate on the event rather than the man, so she said, "It was a first-rate affair. You wouldn't believe the food that was served, or the dishes it was served on, for that matter. It was like being at a five-star restaurant. And the dessert? Sin on a plate."

"Chocolate?" Carole asked.

"You got it."

Carole made a humming sound, but then she was back to the subject at hand. "Okay, so tell me what you thought of the man."

Eve poked through the white takeout carton with a pair of chopsticks, coming out with a peapod.

"Let's see. He can be incredibly overbearing and arrogant. Oh, and he definitely needs to be in control all of the time," she added as she recalled their dance and the jolt it had given him when she'd taken the lead.

She still wasn't sure why she'd done that. She only knew that for some reason she'd felt the need to push him outside the rigid confines of his comfort zone.

"Anything else?" Carole's smile turned knowing. "What did you think of him physically?"

Eve heaved a dramatic sigh. "Okay, he's also seriously gorgeous and just about as sexy as they come."

Carole laughed. "That was what I thought, too. Of course, he was married at the time and I'd just gone through a very ugly divorce. In fact, landing the Burke Financial account helped pay for my lawyer fees among other things," she said wryly. "Officially, Clive hired me, but I worked mainly with Dawson via Rachel Stern."

"Mrs. Stern. That woman needs a hobby."

"She's really not so bad. She's just very protective of Dawson, almost like a second mother," Carole said. "And speaking of mothers, what did you think of Tallulah and the rest of his family?"

Eve grinned. "I liked them all. Very much. They're nice people. Normal. Not at all hoity-toity, if you know what I mean."

"I know."

"Dawson is different around them. He's less..."

stuffy. They obviously love him. That much came through loud and clear."

"The Burkes are a close bunch," Carole agreed.

Eve frowned. "Yes, but he won't shop for them. And he told a friend that he'll be heading out of town at the end of the month to spend the holidays in Cabo San Lucas. From the various comments I overheard, I couldn't help but feel he's avoiding them."

"He's avoiding life and has been since the accident," her friend replied. "In fact, it wasn't until the accident that he added his personal shopping needs to my duties. Before then, I just took care of the business end."

"Sounds like he's really changed."

"Oh, he has." Carole nodded. "Do you feel sorry for him, Eve?"

"Well, of course I do. How can I not? The man lost his wife and daughter."

"Yes. In a car accident on Christmas Eve three years ago." Carole's expression turned grim. "Dawson was the one driving at the time."

"And he was the only one to survive," Eve finished. She closed her eyes, imagining his horror. Her chest ached. "Oh, God."

"Exactly. The Burkes are highly regarded in the community not just because of the business, but because of their overall involvement. In addition to the charity ball, they've got their finger in just about every philanthropic venture that comes along. Dawson's late wife's family is well-known, too, so the accident received plenty of media coverage. There was even some ugly speculation about drunken driving before police revealed that his blood alcohol level had been well below the legal limit."

"How horrible," Eve said.

"Yes," Carole said. "He also was cleared of any negligence. He was driving within the speed limit at the time and, with the exception of that patch of black ice, road conditions were fine."

"It was an accident."

"Yes. An accident. And it could have happened to anyone. Still, from what I've seen and from what those who know him well say, Dawson blames himself."

Of course he does, Eve thought. He was that type of man. Duty, responsibility, family—he took such things very seriously. They were his foundation and in one fell swoop that foundation had been reduced to rubble.

"I really wish you had given me a heads-up, Carole. I'm the first to admit I can be too blunt at times. I might have been a little more diplomatic, a little more sensitive if I'd understood why he needed a personal shopper to purchase gifts for family."

"Actually, that's one of the reasons I didn't tell you," her friend surprised her by saying. "I won't presume to know Dawson well. He's more of a give-orders sort than the sit-down-and-chat kind. But I've always liked him and respected him. And from what I've seen since the accident, he doesn't want coddling or pity. In fact, I'd say those are the last things he needs."

"What does he need?" She hadn't intended to ask that question. In reality, what business was it of hers?

But Carole was smiling coyly when Eve glanced in her direction. "I'm not sure, but maybe someone as resourceful as you will be able to figure it out."

It was half past midnight and though Dawson had gone to bed nearly two hours earlier, he was wide awake. There was nothing new about that. Since the accident he'd had a hard time falling asleep and an even harder time staying asleep once he had. The only time he actually slumbered straight through until morning was when he relied on prescription medication. He didn't like taking that, though. So, instead, he used the wee hours of the morning to make lists of things he needed to do and to catch up on his reading. Sadly, not even the boring article he was scanning in a business journal was making him heavy-eyed this night.

He laid the magazine aside on an oath, turned off the bedside lamp and rolled over. Giving his pillow a couple of punches, he admitted that the insomnia from which he'd suffered for the past several nights was different. He blamed Eve for that.

He also blamed himself.

"I never should have kissed her," he muttered.

Why that mere peck should haunt him, he wasn't sure. At the end of his two dates, he'd kissed both women and with far more intimacy than he had Eve. Yet neither encounter had left him wanting. Quite the opposite.

In the dark, he pictured Eve, her dark eyes wary and going wide as he breached her personal space and settled his mouth over hers. Her lips were soft, inviting. They were tempting, which was why Dawson had ended things quickly. Despite the brief contact, though, he'd felt something he hadn't felt in a very long time: sexually interested.

And alive, his subconscious whispered.

He rolled over and ignored it. "I never should have kissed her," he mumbled a second time.

Yet when he finally drifted off an hour later he dreamed of doing it again, and properly this time.

Eve was preparing to leave for the day when a courier knocked at her door with an official-looking envelope from Burke Financial. She tipped the young man who delivered it and went back inside her apartment to peel back the seal. Then she nearly fell over.

Inside was a pair of theater tickets for the same, sold-out musical that she'd bid on in the silent auction the previous Saturday night, only these were for better seats.

The note read:

Eve,
Burke Financial keeps a box at the theater. No

one was going to this Saturday's performance.
It seemed a shame to let them go to waste.
Enjoy yourself.
Dawson

She called him at his office immediately, and of course got his secretary.

"He has a meeting in half an hour and he's prepping for it," Mrs. Stern informed her. It sounded like a brush-off to Eve. "Can I take a message?"

She's like a second mother, Carole claimed. Eve decided to play on that. Mothers liked nothing better than women with good manners.

"He was kind enough to send me a pair of theater tickets. I just need a moment of his time to thank him properly. Do you think you could put me through?" she asked.

"Just a moment," Mrs. Stern said. Eve was still congratulating herself when Dawson came on the line.

"Hello, Eve."

"Hi. I know you're busy, but I just wanted to call and say thank you."

"I take it the tickets arrived."

"Yes. Just a moment ago. For once I was glad to be running a little behind schedule." As she spoke, she paced the length of her living room in front of the big windows that brought some of the city's skyline inside. "It's incredibly generous of you, Dawson."

"They weren't being used," he replied.

"So you mentioned in your note."

"It seemed a shame for them to go to waste when I knew how much you wanted to see the show."

"Still, I'm grateful, but I find myself in a bit of a quandary." She nibbled her lip.

"And why is that?" he asked.

"Well, I know what these tickets go for. I feel a little awkward accepting something so valuable from a client." Which was partly true.

She pictured Dawson shrugging as he suggested, "Consider it a bonus."

"Thanks, but my commission is all the bonus I require." Eve twisted a lock of hair around her index finger as an idea took shape. "Perhaps you would consider coming to see the play with me?"

The invitation was met with deafening and prolonged silence, making her regret her haste in issuing it.

"Okaaaay. Apparently not. It was just a thought. You've probably already seen the show," she said in an attempt to save face. Not that that was actually possible at this point. "I'll let you get back to work now. Bye." She hung up without giving him a chance to say anything, although she thought she heard him call her name just before she did so.

"God, I'm such an idiot." She groaned in mortification and shuffled backward a couple of steps so she could flop onto the couch.

What had she been thinking, asking him out? The man was probably seriously regretting his generosity right about now. The cordless phone was still in her hand. It trilled to life as she lay amid the throw pillows mentally berating herself. Eve answered it from her prone position.

"Hello?" Home of the Perpetually Foolish, she almost added, and was mighty glad she hadn't when she heard Dawson's voice.

"You hung up awfully fast. I didn't get a chance to give you an answer."

She straightened to sitting, ran a hand through her mussed hair. "I guess I took your silence for an answer."

"Yeah. I'm sorry about that. I was just a little... surprised," he told her.

"I got that," she said. Indeed, it had come through loud and clear.

"When I sent the tickets I assumed you'd have someone else in mind for the second one," he said.

"Such as?" she prodded.

"Such as the date you had to cancel on the night of the ball," he replied.

"Oh, that." Because he couldn't see her expression, she let her grin unfurl. "It was nothing serious. I was just getting together with a friend."

"A friend." He cleared his throat. "And would this friend be male or female?"

"Female."

"Ah."

He was quiet again. Too quiet. Eve began counting. When she got to ten she said, "You're doing it again."

"What?"

"Not saying anything, which forces me to draw my own conclusions."

"And what might those be?" His tone held what sounded like amusement.

Pinching her eyes closed, she gave in to impulse once again. "You're trying to figure out which restaurant you want to take me to for dinner before we head to the theater Friday night."

While Eve held her breath, she heard a mild oath and then strangled laughter. Her lungs felt close to bursting by the time Dawson finally got around to saying, "You're a mind reader."

CHAPTER SEVEN

THE telephone rang as Eve reapplied her lipstick in the mirror that hung by her apartment door. Though it wasn't her style to appear eager, she was wearing her coat and trying not to watch the clock.

"Eve, it's Dawson. Sorry, but I'm running a little behind," he said unnecessarily. She'd expected him to arrive twenty minutes earlier. Their dinner reservation was for six o'clock and that time was fast approaching.

"Everything…okay?" she inquired.

"Wondering if I've changed my mind?"

"I'd understand," she said. And she would, given everything she now knew about his past.

While Eve wasn't considering this a full-fledged date, neither would her conscience allow her to classify it as mere business. She found Dawson interesting, handsome and definitely sexy. Generally speaking, she'd made it a rule not to become personally involved with male clients. But since the Burke account was hers only temporarily courtesy of Carole, she felt safe making an exception.

"I'm not going to stand you up, Eve." His tone was resolute. "Something came up at the last minute."

"Okay. How about I meet you at Tulane then?" she suggested. The restaurant wasn't far from her apartment and it would save him from having to backtrack, as the place was located between them.

He hesitated and Eve was reminded of the fact that he preferred to lead. But then he said, "All right. But give me another fifteen minutes before you leave."

"Okay."

"And, if I'm not there when you arrive, order an appetizer," he added.

"Should I start dinner without you, too?" she asked dryly.

"No. I'll be there."

Dawson walked through the doors at Tulane just as the waiter brought the artichoke dip. He'd shed his overcoat, beneath which he wore a tailored charcoal suit, white shirt and muted print tie. He looked sophisticated, sexy and a tad arrogant as he scanned the tables. When he spotted her, he didn't smile exactly, but his intense expression relaxed even as it brightened. Eve sucked in a breath and exhaled it slowly between her teeth.

"Sorry I'm late," he apologized again as he slipped onto the chair opposite hers.

Her heart rate back to normal, she offered an easy smile. "That's okay."

"I see you ordered an appetizer."

"Yes, hope you like artichoke dip and toast squares," she said.

"You won't hear me complaining."

"I also took a chance and had the waiter bring us some wine." She nodded toward the glass that was in front of Dawson on the table.

He picked it up and took a sip. His brow beetled as his gaze connected with hers. "Pinot noir?"

"It's what you were drinking the other night."

"You certainly pay attention."

Eve picked up her glass and shrugged. "I tend to remember details."

Dawson studied her over the rim of his glass. He remembered details, too. When it came to Eve Hawley, he recalled far too many of them for his own peace of mind.

Details such as the golden flecks that could be teased from her otherwise brown eyes. The candlelight was accomplishing that. And the paleness of her skin that contrasted with a trio of beauty marks at the base of her throat.

She was wearing black tonight. The dress's cut was simple, elegant, and though it sported three-quarter-length sleeves and a rather demure neckline, it was every bit as sexy as the siren-red number she'd had on the other evening. As for her hair, she'd left it down. It hung in a glossy dark cloud of curls around her shoulders. Dawson wondered if it would feel as soft as it looked. If it would smell...

"You're staring at me and not saying anything," Eve said, snapping him out of his stupor. Her full lips bowed when she added, "I'd wonder if I had a piece of artichoke stuck in my teeth, but I haven't tried the dip yet."

Ah, yes, Dawson thought, and then there was that—the woman's surprisingly direct nature. It was another detail, another characteristic, that made her stand out in a crowd. His late wife had been much more reserved and...

He sipped his wine to wash away the memory before it could fully form. No, he wouldn't think of Sheila tonight. He'd done that on his other dates, he realized, spent the time making comparisons, and finding his companions lacking. Both of them had been nice women, but it struck Dawson now how much they had been like his late wife, resembling Sheila in both looks and temperament. Had he unconsciously been seeking a substitute?

Eve was no stand-in. She and Sheila were polar opposites in everything from their personality to their physical characteristics. In fact, he couldn't recall ever being attracted to a woman who was quite so outspoken, independent and vivacious. Making comparisons wouldn't be fair to either woman. Besides, what purpose would they serve? Beyond making Dawson feel guilty.

He took another sip of his wine and swore he felt a couple shackles from the past fall away when he said, "I'm staring because you look lovely this evening."

"Oh." She smiled. "Thank you."

"Actually, I should thank you. I'm glad you asked me to accompany you to the theater tonight."

Her brows rose at that. "Really?"

He set his wine aside. "Yes. I haven't been to the theater in ages."

Her expression turned incredulous. "Do you mean to tell me that your company has access to a pair of choice seats and you don't bother to go?"

"I've been—"

"Busy," she supplied for him, but her overly bright smile told Dawson exactly what she thought of his long-standing excuse.

"I have been busy," he insisted. When his conscience delivered a sharp kick, he admitted, "All right, the truth is I don't get out much these days."

"No, the truth is you don't make *time* to get out much these days," she told him.

Yes, direct.

"They're sort of the same thing."

He thought she might argue, but she let it go and smiled instead. "Well, I suppose I should feel flattered then that you accepted my invitation."

"You're a hard woman to turn down, Eve."

He meant it. He'd spent the past few days wondering why he'd agreed to go. Even amid his many doubts and regrets, though, he hadn't considered canceling on her.

Her smile widened. "I like that answer."

He chuckled. "I thought you might."

The waiter came by to tell them about the evening's dinner specials then. Eve gave the young man her undivided attention, nodding and making appreciative noises as he described the pressed duck.

"Ooh. It sounds wonderful, Danny," she said, flashing a smile that was warm rather than flirtatious.

The woman had a way with people, Dawson thought. It was more than the fact that she treated them with respect. Eve made them feel singled out, special.

After they'd placed their orders and the waiter had gone, Dawson said, "You know, you're very good at that."

"At what?"

"At making people feel like they're important," he replied.

Her brows rose at the same time her chin dipped down. "That's because people *are* important."

He gave a dismissive wave with one hand. "You know what I mean."

"No, I don't. And I'm going to be very disappointed if you suddenly turn into a snob," she informed him. Though she said it lightly, he didn't doubt that she would be.

"I'm not a snob." When she remained silent, he raised a hand palm up as if making a vow. "On my honor, I swear that I'm not. My mother wouldn't allow it."

Eve's expression softened then. "As I've met your mother, not to mention the rest of your lovely family, I have no choice but to believe you."

"Good. And for the record, I intended my observation to be a compliment. A lot of people wouldn't bother to make eye contact with a waiter much less call him by his given name."

"Oh, Danny and I go way back."

"You know him?" Dawson asked, surprised.

She grinned. "We met when I ordered the appetizer." Then she blew out an impatient breath. "Besides, his name was on a badge that was pinned to his shirt. How should I refer to him? 'Hey, you?'"

"Sadly, I know some people who might not refer to him with even that much courtesy."

She shook her head and frowned. "You need to start hanging around with a better class of friends."

"I didn't say they were my friends. I just said I knew such people. They think they're better than everyone else simply because they were born into money."

"Ah, yes." She twirled her wineglass by its stem before taking a sip. Then she surprised him by saying, "I was in a relationship with one of those people for a couple of years, though it took me a while to figure it out."

A couple of years? "It sounds like the two of you were pretty serious."

"I thought so at the time." She selected a piece of toast and scooped up some dip. Before popping it into her mouth, she said, "It turned out that while I was good enough to spend time with, neither he nor his parents felt I had the right pedigree to carry on the bloodlines or some such nonsense."

"Sorry." The evening of the ball, Dawson had sensed vulnerability. Despite her cavalier attitude now, it made an appearance again, and he thought he understood the reason for it.

"Drew did offer to keep seeing me provided that we met discreetly. He said that he had a lot of fun whenever we were together and he hated for that to end."

I bet. "Good for you that you turned him down."

"Well, he made it pretty easy. He'd already announced his engagement to a debutante that it turned out he'd been dating on and off since grad school. Hence the need for discretion." She made a tsking sound and in a rueful voice asked, "Why is it that the other woman is always the last to know?"

"Sorry." He half meant it when he said, "Does this Drew character live around here? Maybe I could go to his house and beat him up for you."

"A tempting offer, but he's back in Connecticut making the rounds with his bride."

"Connecticut?" Dawson frowned. "I thought you said you were from Maine?"

"I said I was born in Maine," she replied. "But I actually grew up in that state and a few others along the eastern seaboard. I ended up in Hartford after college."

"It sounds like you moved around a lot."

"I did." She selected another piece of toast, and he got the feeling that no more information on her childhood would be forthcoming.

"So, I'd have to travel to Connecticut if I wanted to beat up your ex?"

"Nah. He's not worth the price of airfare. Besides, I'm over it."

Over it? Dawson thought as he helped himself to that appetizer. Perhaps Eve was over the man—and he chose not to examine too closely why he hoped that was the case—but she was not over the slight. No, that wound definitely had not healed yet.

"Well, if it's any consolation, it doesn't sound like his marriage will last very long let alone be very happy," Dawson told her.

"No. Probably not." She dabbed her mouth with her napkin, pulling it away to reveal a devilish smile. "I know it's incredibly small of me, but I hope she takes him to the cleaners when they divorce."

"It would serve him right," Dawson agreed. "In my opinion, a man who can't be faithful to a woman deserves to lose something even more, um, personal than money."

Head tilted to one side, Eve grinned at him. "I knew there was a reason I liked you…well, besides your penchant for bubble bath."

"Charity," he replied on a long-suffering sigh, but then he was grinning back.

He liked her, too. She not only made it easy to carry on a conversation, she made it easy to joke. He'd almost forgotten that he possessed a sense of humor. It resurfaced now as he asked, "Do you mean my wit and charm weren't reasons enough?"

"*Witty* and *charming* were not exactly the two adjectives I would have used to describe you at our first meeting." Her eyebrows bobbed. "Even if I did appreciate the view."

Dawson grimaced. "Is it too late to apologize for that?"

"As far as I'm concerned it's never too late to apologize for anything," she replied.

"Very magnanimous of you. In that case, I'm sorry." He decided to come clean. "The truth is I wasn't in the best mood that day. I was hoping to get rid of you."

"I see." She picked up her wine and sipped. "And, what, you thought I'd run screaming in the opposite direction at the sight of a naked man?"

Unfortunately, the waiter picked that exact moment to arrive with their dinner salads. The young man cleared his throat and glanced from Dawson to Eve as he set them on the table.

"Would you care for freshly ground pepper on your salad, miss?" He held out the wooden mill.

"Please," Eve replied, looking not the least bit embarrassed. Dawson, on the other hand, was pretty

sure he'd turned the same color as the raspberry vin-
aigrette dressing that was drizzled over his plate of
mixed baby greens.

"And you, sir?"

Dawson cleared his throat. "No. Thanks."

"Can I get either of you anything else?" the young
man inquired.

"No, Danny." She glanced across the table at
Dawson and winked. "I think we're...covered."

When they were alone again, Dawson said, "Just as
a point of clarification, I was not naked when we met."

"Oh, that's right." But Eve caused him to blush all
over again when she added, "You were wearing a
sheet. I guess I let my imagination fill in the parts it
concealed."

On a strangled laugh, Dawson replied, "I hope
your imagination did me justice."

"I don't think you need to be concerned on that
score."

"I guess we'll see."

His response and what it implied had both of them
sobering. By the time Danny returned with their
entrees they had returned to far safer topics of conversation than Dawson's anatomy.

As they left the restaurant an hour later, Eve got an idea.

"You know, my Tahoe is in the parking ramp. Why
don't you give your driver the rest of the night off? I
can take us to the theater." She sent him an angelic

smile. "I promise to be a perfect gentleman and drop you at your home well before you turn into a pumpkin."

Dawson glanced toward the curb where the limousine was waiting. His omnipresent driver had already hopped out to open the rear door for them.

She braced for his protest, but he agreed.

"All right. I guess that makes more sense than taking separate vehicles to the theater."

Even more surprising than his agreement was the fact that Dawson didn't insist on getting behind the wheel when they reached her Tahoe. Without a word, he got in on the passenger's side…after opening the driver's door for her, of course. If she saw his mother again, Eve would be sure to compliment Tallulah on her son's fine manners.

"I'm not sure I've ever met a man who was willing to relinquish the driver's seat, especially to a woman," she joked after starting the vehicle.

She glanced over at Dawson in the Tahoe's dim interior. Far from smiling, his face was drawn, his lips compressed. He was a man who preferred to be in control at all times, yet not only was he willing to let her drive, but it also dawned on Eve that he paid someone else to do the driving for him on a regular basis. Before, Eve had considered that a wealthy man's preference. He could afford such a luxury and so he enjoyed it. It struck her now that, as the survivor of a harrowing crash, hiring a driver really was more of a necessity.

To fill the awkward silence, she said, "Well, just to put your mind at ease, I've never had so much as a traffic ticket."

"Good to know," came his clipped response.

Out of the corner of her eye, she watched him buckle his seat belt and then pull on the strap as if testing it. Afterward, he rested the palms of his hand on his thighs, hardly the picture of relaxation. In the rear of a limo it was probably easy to forget about oncoming traffic. That wasn't the case with a front seat view.

"It's nice to leave the driving to other people once in a while, isn't it?" she said in an effort to make small talk.

Dawson responded with a tight-lipped, "Yes."

"You probably get a lot done on the morning commute."

"Yes." Another laconic reply.

"I'd love to be able to while away my drive time reading or whatnot. I try to time it so I'm not on the roads at the height of rush hour. Traffic can be a killer, especially on the area highways." As soon as the words were out she wanted to snatch them back. If Eve hadn't needed to keep her foot on the gas pedal, she would have used it to kick herself. Talk about a poor choice of words.

Dawson, however, answered with an honest, "Yes. The highways can be a real killer."

"My God, Dawson. I'm sorry. That came out badly."

"No need to apologize."

"You told me before that you don't like to talk about the accident." She refrained from adding that he probably should, rather than keeping all of that pain and self-blame bottled up inside. Her thoughts turned to her father, a perpetual man-child who had been emotionally stunted by his grief. It wasn't healthy, Eve knew.

"We weren't talking about the accident," he said. "And we're not."

"Dawson—"

"We're talking about driving. I prefer to leave that job to other people, which is why I pay a driver."

She allowed him the out, though they both knew he was lying. "Ah. Right. Well, I live for the day I can not only afford to hire a driver but also pay someone to clean my toilets. It's a nasty chore."

"I'll have to take your word for it," he replied blandly.

"Do you mean to tell me you've never scrubbed a commode?" she asked.

"Never."

"Well, I take care of mine every Saturday morning if you ever feel the need to rack up another life experience," she offered.

As she turned onto Curtis Street, she glanced over in time to see his lips loosen with the beginnings of a smile.

"Thanks, but no," he said.

CHAPTER EIGHT

WHEN they left the theater a few hours later, Eve was humming one of the musical's more upbeat tunes.

"I take it you enjoyed the show," Dawson said as they made their way to her Tahoe.

"I loved it." She sighed. "Thank you again for coming with me."

"You're welcome. You know, that's the third time I've seen *Les Miz*. The first two times were years ago when it was on Broadway."

"You're kidding."

He shook his head.

"You must love it."

Actually, he hadn't really cared for it in the past. Tonight, he had. Dawson credited Eve for that. She had a way of making him loosen up and let go. She'd laughed at the ribald antics of the Thénardiers and cried as Jean Valjean made his passionate plea to God to spare Marius's life. At times, he'd found himself more interested in watching her than the stage.

"Do you own the soundtrack, too?" she asked, pulling him from his introspection.

"No."

"You should have bought a copy tonight. I can lend you mine, if you'd like," she offered.

"Thanks, but I'll pass. The music is outstanding, don't get me wrong. But it's not my style."

"Oh?"

"I'm more a vintage rock fan. You know, pounding bass and wicked guitar riffs. Something to get the blood pumping."

Eve smiled at him and he swallowed as the phrase took on a new meaning.

"Blood pumping, right." She nodded as if in agreement, but shattered the illusion by adding, "Don't forget men with seriously bad hairstyles wearing spandex and screaming out indecipherable lyrics at the tops of their lungs."

She had a point about the bad hair and spandex. He tucked his hands deep into the pockets of his overcoat. "I can figure out the lyrics."

When she tipped down her chin and arched her brows, he amended, "Most of the time."

As they started walking again, Eve mused, "I once dreamed about a career on Broadway. My goal was to be cast as Belle in the stage production of *Beauty and the Beast*. I had all of the songs memorized, and I rehearsed them daily in front of the bathroom mirror."

"So, you have a good singing voice?"

She shook her head. "I can't carry a tune, which is pretty much what killed that choice of careers for me."

Dawson chuckled. "I suppose that would nip things in the bud. How old were you at the time?"

"Eleven. My dad's a musician."

It was one of the few references she'd made to her family, he realized. He found he wanted to know more. "Really? What kind?"

"The wanna-be kind. He plays old-school rock," she replied. There was an edge to her tone he hadn't heard before.

"Hence your objection to the genre."

She merely shrugged.

"So, you wanted to follow in your dad's footsteps," Dawson said.

Eve snorted indelicately. "Only if they led me right to him. He was away. A lot," she added. "Actually, my goal was to become a major stage star, an unrivaled success. I wanted my name in lights, as the saying goes."

It was pretty easy for Dawson to read between the lines. "You wanted your father's attention."

"Sure I did. Sometimes I still do. There's nothing unusual about that. All kids want their parents' attention," she stated matter-of-factly, but he noted the stiff set to her shoulders, the furrow in her brow.

Yes, all children wanted their parents' attention, but not all of them got it. Dawson had been lucky in that regard. He'd had it in spades. Still did, come to think of it. Eve? Apparently not.

They reached the Tahoe and she redirected the conversation. "So, what did you want to be when you were growing up?"

Dawson opened the driver's door for her before heading around to the passenger side. Once seated, he replied, "Do you mean before I figured out that I didn't look so good in long hair and spandex, or after I accepted the fact that the National Football League wasn't going to come recruiting?"

Her lips twitched as she started the ignition. "Either-or. Surprise me."

He scrubbed a hand over his chin, thinking. "Well, I pretty much always knew I'd go into the family business. It suited my personal interests, not to mention my academic strengths. I didn't feel pressured to do it or anything." Dawson leaned back in his seat, relaxing a little as he recalled the advice his father had given him just before he'd gone off to college. *Do what makes you happy, son. Not what you think will make me happy.* "My dad would have understood if I had chosen a different career. My grandfather would have been livid, but Dad...he would have understood."

He smiled after saying it, feeling warm even though the Tahoe had yet to heat up.

"The two of you seem really close," Eve noted.

"We are. Yes." He cleared his throat, a little embarrassed to have been lost in nostalgia. Memories had been his nemesis for the past few years, proving so hurtful that he'd blocked out the good along with the bad.

Ahead, a traffic light turned red. After stopping, Eve turned to face him. "I know this is none of my business, but I'm going to ask anyway. If the two of you are so close, why are you estranged?"

The question left Dawson staggered. "We're not estranged," he said.

Eve's gaze remained steady as she said, "Then why are you spending the holidays in Cabo rather than with your family here?"

I don't have a family, he thought. Sheila, Isabelle, they were gone and he was alone. But he knew they weren't the family to which Eve was referring. "It's...complicated."

"I don't doubt that," she replied. "Life tends to get that way from time to time for everyone. That's especially true after a tragedy. But it sure seems like you're punishing them."

"You're wrong. Way, way off base." He shook his head vehemently as his throat seemed to close. Eve was mistaken in her assessment. If he was punishing anyone, it wasn't his parents and sister. He was punishing himself.

"That's the way it seems."

"That's because you don't understand," he said.

Nobody did. They hadn't been trapped inside that crumpled-up car while emergency workers tried unsuccessfully to revive his wife. They hadn't been the ones pleading with firefighters to hurry as they finally managed to free his daughter from her safety restraint in the mangled backseat.

In the Tahoe's dimly lit interior her expression radiated sincerity when she invited, "Then help me understand, Dawson. Better yet, help *them* understand."

"I…" But the words remained stubbornly lodged in his throat. The only ones to finally make it free were, "The traffic light is green."

Eve parked the Tahoe in the circular drive in front of Dawson's home. The rest of the ride from the theater had been accomplished in strained silence. She accepted the blame for that. She shouldn't have pushed him so hard.

She wasn't sure exactly why she'd done it, except that she'd hoped by talking about the accident he would finally see that it was just that—an accident. She wanted him to accept what everyone else knew. Dawson was as much a victim, a casualty, as his late wife and little daughter.

"Here we are," she said. "I know I've already thanked you for the tickets, but I want to do so again. I had a nice time tonight, Dawson."

"You're welcome. I did, too."

"I'm glad you're still able to say that. I'm sorry about…" She waved a hand, opting not to plow that rocky ground a second time.

He caught her fingers and gave them a gentle squeeze. "Let's forget about that, okay?"

Eve didn't think forgetting was wise. Indeed, it was at the crux of his problem. But for the moment she agreed. No more pushing tonight. She smiled. "All right."

Dawson had yet to release her hand. Though they both wore gloves, she swore she could feel the heat from his skin warming hers through two layers of lined leather.

His thumb began to rub the palm of her hand. She'd never considered her palm or any other place on her hand to be an erogenous zone. It turned out she was wrong. Way wrong.

Eve swallowed a moan and stammered, "S-so, should I walk you to your front door? I promised to be a gentleman, after all."

"No need for that."

The palm caress continued. "Mmm-kay," she managed to say.

"If you walk me to my door, I'd only feel obligated to walk you back to your car afterward." One side of his mouth lifted. "Can't let you be the only gentleman."

"Well, I guess I'd better stay here then. Otherwise it sounds like we could pass the entire night walking back and forth between my Tahoe and your front porch."

"That would make for a long night."

"Very long," she agreed.

"And it's cold outside."

"Below freezing." She shivered, though the reaction had less to do with Denver's current temperature than the ministrations of his thumb.

"We'd have to move fast to stay warm," he said. In contrast the smile he offered was slow, seductive.

"If we jogged, I suppose it could be considered aerobic exercise."

"Exercise, hmm?" His thumb stopped moving and Dawson released her hand. Gaze steady, expression serious, he removed his gloves, tugging one finger free at a time. Anticipation hummed until he reached for her across the vehicle's console. Big, warm hands framed her face, drew her forward.

"I can think of more interesting methods of increasing my heart rate while in the company of a beautiful woman," he murmured just before kissing her.

Soft. That was Eve's first thought. Though so much of the man was hard and uncompromising, his lips were soft, their pressure gentle. She thought he might end things as quickly as he had the night of the ball, leaving her to wonder and to want. He didn't.

"Eve." Dawson whispered her name as he changed the angle of their mouths.

His hands were in her hair now, fingers weaving through it. Slow? Soft? Nothing about the man's demeanor fit these descriptions now. *Urgent* was the word that came to mind as he fumbled with the fat buttons of her wool coat. She shifted in her seat to improve his access, her elbow catching on the steering wheel. The horn blasted loudly, blowing a hole right through the intimacy of the moment. Romance took a backseat to reality.

Eve sucked in a breath as Dawson pulled away. Her body was sizzling, snapping like an exposed electrical wire. Had she ever been this turned on? A glance in Dawson's direction had her swallowing the suggestive remark she'd been about to make. He was slumped back in his seat, scrubbing a hand over his face.

Regrets.

She could see them as clearly as if they had been tattooed on his forehead, hear them even though he had yet to say a word. Eve closed her eyes, mentally kicked herself. To think for a moment she'd thought the only thing that had come between them during that passionate exchange had been the vehicle's console and their layers of clothing.

"You're not ready for…this. Are you?"

His laughter was brittle, bitter. "That's not exactly the issue at the moment."

"I'm not talking physically, Dawson."

"No." He swore, stared straight ahead and admitted, "I don't know."

"It's okay," she assured him, even as her own heart began to ache a bit.

"It's not okay!" He cursed again, this time with more force, and turned to face her. She saw anger and frustration, neither of which was directed at her. "None of this is okay, Eve. None of it."

His strident words seemed to echo in the vehicle. She remained silent, waiting for him to continue. After a long moment, he did. His tone was missing its angry edge. Now Dawson just sounded tired and a little lost when he told her, "Some people are able to just go with the flow. Not me. I had my life all figured out, you know? I made plans and then I followed through on them."

"You're talking about before the accident?"

"Yes. I made plans," he said a second time.

Of course, he had. Dawson was the sort of man who needed to take charge, to be in control. But tragedy and grief wouldn't follow orders. On the contrary. Once they were on the scene, they called the shots.

"It's time to make new plans," Eve said softly.

He faced her, his gaze glittering hard in the meager glow cast by the landscaping lights. "I did. After the accident I made new plans. I've been living my life according to them ever since."

She swallowed. "And?"

"You seem to be botching them up, Eve."

Her mouth fell open. Before she could ask what he meant by that potent statement, however, Dawson was opening the door and getting out of the Tahoe. He slammed it shut without another word.

It was several minutes after he disappeared inside the house before she felt steady enough to drive away.

The weekend proved long, as did the following week. Dawson had plenty of work to keep him busy and he finalized his plans for his trip to Cabo San Lucas. Eve called a couple times, but he made excuses not to speak with her.

You're not ready for this, are you?

That damned question seemed to taunt him.

He was glad when Friday dawned. Another week down. Just two more to go until he boarded that plane and left everything familiar. Then he glanced out the window, saw the snow and cursed. The forecast had called for it, so the accumulation blanketing his lawn hardly came as a surprise. Even so, he didn't like it. After showering and dressing in more casual clothes than he would wear to the office, he headed downstairs to his study. As he always did on days when the weather turned inclement, he would work from home.

As a child, he'd loved the white stuff and not just because if enough of it fell he got the day off from school. No, he'd loved playing in it, making forts out of it and packing it into balls for fights with his friends. Even as an adult he hadn't minded it, though it often presented a headache during his commute to or from work.

What had turned him off completely to winter

weather, of course, was the accident, which is why he'd opted to work from home this day.

It came as an absolute shock then when, halfway through the afternoon, his housekeeper tapped at his door to announce he had a guest.

"Eve Hawley is here," Ingrid said.

Leather creaked as he settled back in his chair. He didn't want to see her and yet he did.

"Send her in, please."

She appeared in the doorway a moment later, smiling apologetically and looking lovely enough to snatch his breath away.

"Sorry to disturb you."

"That's all right." He rested his elbows on the desk blotter and steepled his fingers in front of him. "Did we have an appointment?" he asked.

"No. Actually, I wasn't expecting to see you at all. I figured you would be at your office."

Once his ego had absorbed the blow, he replied, "I decided to work from home today."

"So I see."

"What can I do for you, Eve?" he asked curtly.

He saw hurt flash in her dark eyes just before she blinked, and hated himself for it. This wasn't her fault. None of this was her fault.

"I have some gift ideas as well as some actual things that I purchased for family members. I was planning to leave them for you to look over."

"Okay."

At that single, sparse word, she backed up a step, nodding. None of the spunk she'd exhibited on her first visit to his home was evident when she said, "Well, I'll just leave them with Ingrid. Thanks."

She'd already turned and gone before Dawson managed to launch himself from his seat. He caught up with her in the front foyer just as she was pulling on her jacket.

"Eve, wait."

She turned, a manufactured smile tilting up her lips. "Yes?"

He closed his eyes and shook his head. "Don't go. Not like this."

"Like what?"

"Angry."

"I'm not angry. Why in the world would I be angry?" she asked, tossing the end of her scarf over one shoulder.

"Because I was being a jerk."

She stopped in the process of pulling on her gloves. "Yes," she agreed with a considering nod. "You were. A rude jerk to be precise."

Dawson's laughter was strained, even though the ice had been broken. "You don't believe in cutting a guy any slack, do you?"

"To what purpose?"

He ran his tongue over the outside of his top teeth. "Okay, how about this? Do you have any plans for dinner?"

"Tonight?" she inquired.

The woman was definitely playing hardball.

"Yes, tonight."

"Hmm. Let me think." She tapped her lower lip with the tip of one gloved index finger. "Not exactly, although I did take a chicken breast out of the freezer to thaw."

It was a bit of a blow to learn he could lose out to poultry. "I believe Ingrid is making a pork roast."

"Ah, the other white meat," she said, repeating the industry's slogan.

"Yes. She's a very good cook," he added in the hopes of aiding his cause.

Eve eyed him stoically. "Is that an invitation, Dawson?" she asked.

"It is."

"I see."

She was silent for so long that he was forced to ask, "Does that mean you accept?"

She tilted her head to one side. "Depends."

"On what?"

"On what else is on the menu," she said.

He cleared his throat. "I'm not sure. Probably some sort of rice or potato dish and a vegetable. Maybe a salad. Do you have a preference? I can let Ingrid know and I'm sure she'll try to accommodate it," he offered.

"Actually, I meant in the way of conversation."

"Oh."

She folded her arms over her chest. "Are you going to talk to me?"

"Of course I am," he replied, somewhat indignant.

"I mean an actual conversation, Dawson. No chitchat about the weather or diatribes on the economy. I can get that watching the news while I eat Chinese takeout."

He blew out a breath. "Good God, Eve. You're a hard woman to please."

She unzipped the quilted down jacket she wore and laid it over his arm. Her smile was purely female when she replied, "You don't know the half of it."

CHAPTER NINE

SINCE they had some time to kill before dinner was served, Dawson suggested they sit in the great room where a fire blazed cheerfully in the hearth. Eve agreed and he helped her carry in the purchases she'd made.

In the past, he'd given Carole carte blanche to buy his family's gifts. Afterward, he hadn't wanted anything to do with them. Eve, of course, insisted on running everything past him.

"At the very least you should know what you bought so that when they thank you, you won't appear baffled."

"I'm never baffled," he responded. Her brows rose fractionally as if to say, "Right."

"Another one of your principles?" he asked.

"Exactly."

As they sat on the sofa and went through the goods she'd brought with her, Dawson was impressed. The woman had a good eye. She'd pegged his mother's taste perfectly with a specially designed amethyst ring that was surrounded by smaller stones. Tallulah was going to love it. He told Eve as much.

She smiled, looking pleased. "That was my thought, too. As for your dad, he was difficult. I went out on a limb with this since it cannot be returned, but since Clive seemed to be a real hockey fan, I thought he might appreciate it."

She pulled a red game jersey from the bag that was on her lap.

"That's Gordie Howe's number," Dawson said as he reached for it. "He was one of the all-time greats."

"It's a vintage National Hockey League sweater and it's signed. I know the Wings aren't your father's favorite team, but the Avalanche wasn't around back in the day." Her tone turned wry. "I know this because I made a fool of myself in a sports memorabilia store downtown."

Dawson chuckled. "Dad's going to love it. He'll argue, of course, that Ted Lindsay was actually the better player, but he'll love it. Thank you."

She rifled through another bag as he folded the jersey and set it aside.

"And here's the Misty Stark purse I mentioned getting for your sister. I went with something medium-sized from the designer's spring collection."

"This spring?"

"I know someone who knows someone who owed

that someone a really big favor." She let out a sigh that was purely feminine. "Lisa's going to love it."

The handbag reminded Dawson of a pastel-colored sausage with handles. "I'll have to take your word for it," he said dryly.

"I'm still looking for something for your brother-in-law. Suggestions at this point would be appreciated. Christmas is only two weeks away."

"I'll give it some thought," he replied.

"Maybe you could call your sister, pick her brain a little," she suggested. "Or you could go to Sunday dinner this week and talk to her there."

"I…I'll see what I can do."

"Okay. Thanks." She leaned forward then to pull a large and very heavy shopping bag across the Turkish rug. "And now for the coup de grâce."

"What is it?"

"Take a peek."

He felt a bit like a kid himself when he did. Inside was the gaming system Brian and Colton had been raving about the night of the ball.

"No way!" Dawson said on a startled laugh. "I know you said you could get this for the boys, but… How on earth did you manage it?"

"Trade secret." She offered a cagey smile. "I can't give you specifics, but I can assure you that no laws were broken."

"The boys are going to love this." He grinned at her. "You're something else."

Eve focused her attention back on the bag. "I also picked up a few age-appropriate games to go with it that I think they will enjoy."

Of course she had. The woman was nothing if not thorough. "You think of everything."

"It's my job," she said lightly. "Besides, after the chemistry set fiasco I felt you needed to really go all out to reestablish yourself as a 'cool' uncle."

He rubbed the back of his neck and offered a sheepish, "Thanks."

Though he'd known it all along, it hit him suddenly that he wouldn't be there to watch the boys open this gift. He wouldn't be there to see any of his family members open their gifts. Just as he hadn't been at his parents' house on Christmas Day last year or the year before or…

As if she'd read his mind, Eve said, "It's a shame you won't be in town to see the boys tear into this. They're going to be so excited."

While his family gathered around a decorated Douglas fir tree, joking, laughing and exchanging presents, he would be alone in Cabo, as far away from snow and holiday merriment as he could possibly manage. Dawson pictured himself sitting poolside at the condo he'd rented, a tall glass of something chilled and fortified in one hand to help blot out the memories.

Eve was watching him, apparently waiting for him to say something in response. He gave a negligent shrug. "I'll catch up with them after the holidays."

"Okay. Terrific." She nodded. He didn't trust her easy agreement and for good reason. "You can see them at a Sunday dinner at your parents' house."

"Eve—"

She cut him off by slapping her knee in exaggerated fashion. "Oh, wait, I forgot. You don't go to Sunday dinners at your parents' house any longer."

"Are you trying to make me feel bad?" he asked tightly. "I can assure you, there's no need. I already do."

Instead of apologizing, Eve said, "Good, then you understand exactly how your loved ones feel when you shut them out and stand them up not just on the holidays but on a regular basis throughout the year."

On an oath, he launched to his feet. Irritation and guilt blended together, proving to be a volatile mix. "Didn't your mother ever tell you that it's not polite to poke around in people's private affairs?" he snapped.

"No. She didn't." Eve stood as well. "My mother died of a drug overdose when I was eight."

He blanched. "God. I…I'm sorry."

"No." She kneaded her forehead. "I'm sorry. I played that like a damned trump card and it was a lousy thing to do. But I'm not sorry for poking around in your private affairs, as you put it."

"Why does this matter to you?" he demanded.

"Because…because it…" Her next words nipped his anger in the bud. "Because *you* matter to me, Dawson. Okay? You matter."

"Eve." He closed his eyes and shook his head,

unable or unwilling to process the emotions her words evoked. Or maybe he was just too afraid. After all, it was hard to cling tightly to the past when a part of him wanted to start reaching for the future.

"I probably shouldn't tell you that," she said quietly. He opened his eyes in time to watch her swallow and cross her arms over her chest. The move struck him as defensive rather than defiant, especially when she added, "Unfortunately, I have a very bad habit of leading with my heart where men are concerned. Just don't let it go to your head."

"I don't know what to say," he replied, though the truth was that Eve mattered to him, too. Indeed, in a very short period of time, she'd managed to thoroughly shake up the status quo of Dawson's otherwise rigidly ordered life. He still wasn't sure he liked it.

"Don't say anything. I prefer to do all the talking anyway." She pushed the hair back from her face and expelled a deep breath. "As my bombshell of a moment ago should make perfectly clear to you, I don't come from the kind of family you do. After my mother died, my father took off and I was shuttled around from one relative to another, all of whom made it plain that they disapproved of my dad, had been disappointed in my mother and didn't have very high hopes that I'd amount to much."

"Aw, Eve."

"Don't feel sorry for me. That's not the purpose

behind my words. You're lucky, Dawson. Very lucky to have people who care about you and who want to remain close."

"I'm sorry."

"Don't be sorry for me. I've accepted my family for what it is and my father for what he isn't. He's let grief and regrets rule and ruin his life. I don't want to see you make the same mistake." She blinked a couple of times in rapid succession and managed a smile. "Okay, that's all I'm going to say on either subject."

Dawson didn't quite believe her. But before he could think of anything to say in response, Ingrid arrived in the doorway.

"Dinner is ready, Mr. Burke."

Dawson's formal dining room sported vaulted ceilings, a crystal chandelier and an oval cherry table that could comfortably accommodate a dozen guests. A gas fireplace and glowing candle centerpiece made the large room cozy. But it was the framed family portrait hanging over the mantel that made it personal.

Eve had never seen photographs of Dawson's late wife and daughter, but even if he hadn't been included in the shot, she would have known who the other two people were. In an odd way, she recognized them, even if she did not recognize the happy, relaxed man who was seated with them.

As Ingrid set out serving dishes heaped with enough steaming food to serve a small army, Eve discreetly studied the photograph. Sheila was blond-haired and blue-eyed with the delicate beauty of a porcelain doll. Isabelle was lovely, too. Eve glimpsed mischief in the little girl's light eyes and a hint of her father's stubbornness in her small jaw. She'd expected them to be beautiful and they were. But what truly surprised Eve was the odd connection she felt to Dawson's loved ones and the disappointment that they would never meet.

The dinner conversation started out stilted and strained thanks to the emotionally charged discussion that had preceded it. She blamed herself for that. What had she been thinking, provoking the man and then essentially baring her soul to him?

No matter, the deed was done and she wouldn't waste her time or energy regretting it now. Besides, she'd only spoken the truth. Dawson *did* matter to her. Eve hadn't realized how much until the words had tumbled out.

Oh, well. She was who she was…though it seemed she never learned. No, she picked up stakes and started over, but she never learned.

She was fussing with her napkin when Dawson asked, "Would you care for some wine?"

Eve pushed her glass closer to his side of the table. "Yes, but just a little, please."

Once he'd poured the chilled pinot grigio, dinner

became a far more relaxed affair. It had nothing to do with the loosening effects of alcohol, but the fact that Dawson spilled his wine down the front of his shirt when he went to take a sip.

It was an accident, of that Eve was sure. He wasn't the sort of man given to slapstick comedy, though he had loosened up considerably since their first meeting. Had that been a mere two weeks ago?

"I can't believe I did that." He dabbed at his shirt front with his napkin. "I'm rarely so clumsy."

"It's my fault," Eve said.

He stopped wiping and glanced over at her. "How do you figure that?"

Face straight, she replied, "It's the effect I have on men. They become blundering fools in my presence."

Dawson snorted. And though he was smiling, he sounded somewhat serious when he replied, "You certainly do have an effect on me, Eve."

Half an hour later, Eve pushed back from the table on a contented sigh. "I probably should have passed on that second helping of pork tenderloin, but it was too good."

"Irresistible," he agreed as he watched Eve dab her mouth with a linen napkin.

Heat curled inside her at the suggestive remark. Just over his right shoulder, Sheila and Isabelle smiled down at Eve from the portrait, dousing any flames before they could start. Just as well, she decided. Just as well.

During the meal, while they'd talked companionably, steering clear of weighty or emotionally complicated topics, the candles on the table had burned low and the sun had set outside. Though Eve had planned to leave as soon as good manners would allow once they'd finished eating, she glanced out the window and reevaluated.

"Let's go for a walk, work off some of these calories," she suggested instead.

"A walk? It's snowing," he said.

"Yes, I hear it does that in Denver. No need to worry. I won't melt." Her eyebrows arched. "Or are you afraid that you will?"

"It's getting dark, Eve."

Dawson's home was surrounded by a private, almost parklike setting with mature trees and meandering paths. "The landscape lighting looks adequate for a leisurely stroll."

"The paths haven't been shoveled recently. A good three inches have fallen since the grounds crew went through last."

She batted that excuse aside, too. "That's all right. I've got boots."

Of course, the boots in question were unlined and made of supple Italian leather with three-inch heels that hardly made them suitable for a hike—or even a stroll—in inclement weather, but she was willing to take her chances.

"I don't know."

Like a veteran poker player, Eve upped the ante. "I promise to protect you."

But it was Dawson who called. "Maybe I'm not the one who needs protecting."

"Is that a threat?" she inquired.

He set aside his napkin and pushed back from the table. Gaze direct and challenging, he said, "There's only one way to find out. Are you still game?"

"Please." She snorted. "That question is insulting. I've never backed down from a challenge."

"I didn't think you had." One side of his mouth lifted, tugging her pulse rate right along with it. "I'll just get our coats."

Outside, the air was crisp. It stole Eve's breath, making her glad for the scarf that she'd wound around her neck. She tucked her chin into it now.

"It's lovely here," she commented. And it was. Winter had wrought its magic, covering everything in a pristine layer of white that sparkled like diamonds in the moonlight.

"The grounds were what attracted me to this property in the first place," Dawson admitted.

"I can see why."

"If you think it's lovely now, you should see it in the spring or summer. The flowerbeds are incredible."

"I wouldn't have taken you for a green thumb."

"Oh, it's black, believe me. I know my limits, which is why I hired the services of a professional."

She chuckled. "The economy loves people who know their limits since it helps create all sorts of job opportunities."

"Like professional shoppers?"

"Exactly."

"Well, I'm glad to do my part for my country." His voice grew soft. "I haven't walked out here in the winter in…a long time."

Eve figured she knew exactly how long, so she remained silent.

After a moment, he added, "I used to love the winter. I looked forward to the first snowfall."

"Me, too." She scuffed her foot along the walkway, ruffling the blanket of white, before bending down to scoop up a handful. "Snow made everything seem so clean, so perfect," she said as she compacted the snow into a ball.

"And your life wasn't perfect."

"No. But whose is?" She shrugged off the melancholy of childhood memories and changed the subject. "You know, this is really good packing snow."

"So I see. Are you thinking of making a snowman or something?"

"Or something." When she smiled his eyes narrowed.

"You wouldn't."

"Wouldn't what?" she asked innocently.

He backed up a couple of steps. "You wouldn't throw that thing at me."

"And if I do?"

He folded his arms. "You do and you'll be asking for trouble."

"Dawson, Dawson," Eve said, shaking her head. "What did I tell you about me and challenges?"

"That you never back—" The snowball hit him in the chest before he could finish. He gaped at her. "I can't believe you just did that."

Eve bent down and scooped up a second handful. "Then this is going to come as a complete shock," she said, tossing the snow right into his face.

Her laughter followed the ball's flight path, but her mirth was short-lived. Dawson didn't even pause to wipe it off before he launched himself in her direction. She feinted right to avoid him and managed to get a full ten feet up the path before he caught up with her, grabbing her around her waist. Eve skidded on the walk, betrayed by her boots. Both she and Dawson wound up going down. Snow cushioned her fall. Snow and man. Somehow she wound up partway on top of him.

"Are you okay?" he asked.

"I think I broke my heel."

"Are you in pain?"

She laughed as she clarified, "The heel of my boot. It got caught on something. What are you doing, anyway? We were supposed to be having a snowball fight."

"We still are." And with that he brought up his

snow-filled hand and rubbed it over her cheek. It wasn't only the cold that had her shivering. Dawson had shifted so that he was now mostly on top of her.

"You know, when I was a kid I didn't believe in taking any prisoners. But I've decided to make an exception in your case. You're too pretty to annihilate."

"So, I'm your prisoner."

"Yes."

"Hmm." She pulled a considering face. "I guess this isn't so bad."

"That's because the torture hasn't begun yet." His gaze was on her lips.

"Torture?" she repeated in a husky voice she barely recognized as her own. "What kind of torture?"

"This," he whispered just before his mouth met hers.

CHAPTER TEN

DAWSON could think of a million reasons why he should stop the kiss before it progressed any further. First among them was the fact that he and Eve were outside lying on the snow-covered ground. She apparently didn't mind. When he started to pull away, she wrapped her arms around his neck and held him in place, taking where a moment ago she'd been the one giving.

Her arms weren't the only thing wrapped around him. Her legs were, too. One was hooked over his calf, the other angled over his thigh, anchoring him in place. Their bodies fit together perfectly. He could tell that despite the layers of their clothes, and it fueled both his imagination and his desire.

It had been a long time—a very long time— since he'd lain atop of woman. His body had no trouble remembering the pleasure. Need surged through him with tsunami force, shredding his control until it hung by a thread. Though Dawson knew he was playing with fire, he rocked forward slightly anyway.

Eve moaned.

He did it again.

This time they both moaned, and that last frayed thread of his control snapped. It was only when Eve's icy hands moved beneath jacket and sweater and came into contact with the bare skin just above the waistband of his jeans that reality came slamming back.

"This is insane," he said as he came up for air.

There didn't seem to be enough of it, especially when he glanced down at Eve. She was still lying in the snow, dark hair fanning out around her head. In the moonlight her eyes glowed with an arousing mix of awareness and humor.

"Absolutely insane," she agreed on a chuckle. "My butt is numb."

Parts of Dawson had lost all feeling, too. Unfortunately, his back wasn't one of them. He discovered this when he levered away from Eve and rolled to one side. Long into the night, and in more ways than one, he would be paying for this spontaneous and very sensual tussle.

Grimacing as he rose, he reached down to help Eve to her feet.

"Are you okay?" she asked.

"I will be." After a couple or four painkillers. He'd also be calling Wanda for a therapeutic massage first thing in the morning.

They entered the house through the French doors that led from the patio directly into the kitchen. Dawson always hated entering the house in the evening when his staff had gone home. The place was so quiet and seemed so…lifeless. Eve chased away the gloom by stamping her feet and giving her damp hair a toss.

"Ingrid has gone home for the night, but I can make some coffee or a cup of tea, if you'd like."

"Your housekeeper doesn't live here?"

"No."

"What about your driver?" she asked.

"His rooms are over the garage."

"And that masseuse I saw the first day?" she asked as she removed her scarf and unzipped her jacket.

He chuckled ruefully. "At the moment I wish she lived here, but no. I prefer my privacy."

"Nothing wrong with privacy," she agreed. After tucking her scarf into the sleeve of her jacket, she draped it around the back of one chair. "Do you have any hot chocolate?"

"I…don't know. Possibly."

"I'd prefer that to tea or coffee if you have it. Chocolate in any form trumps all else," she said.

"My sister has made the same claim."

"Ooh, and little marshmallows. I love those little marshmallows."

"I can't make any promises, but I'll do my best to accommodate your request. In the meantime, we probably should get out of these wet clothes."

"Hmm." She tapped her lips with an index finger.

"What?" he asked as he put his coat on the back of another chair.

"I'm trying to decide if you're being chivalrous with that suggestion or merely clever," Eve said.

He smiled. "A man can be both."

"Okay, you can prove that by helping me out of these boots. The leather is wet and they feel like they've become a second skin." She took a seat and smiled up at him, managing to look prim and provocative at the same time.

He knelt because it was warranted and pushed up the damp hem of one pant leg so he could find the zipper on the side of the boot. The leather was high quality and soaked. He had a bad feeling her boots might be ruined.

"These aren't exactly practical footwear for Denver winters," he said.

"No, but they're sexy as hell."

She had a point. It took a little effort, but Dawson managed to free the boot from her foot. Though she hadn't asked him to, he peeled off the damp stocking beneath it, revealing a set of chilly pink toes whose nails were painted fire-engine-red. He rubbed the foot between his hands, chafing some warmth into it and hoping to cool down his libido in the process. Since his first days of dating, he'd had a thing for red toenails on members of the opposite sex. He wasn't sure why. Something about them screamed sexy.

That was especially true in the winter when no one else was likely to see them. It made this glimpse more intimate and almost like a secret.

He groaned.

"Is your back giving you trouble?" Eve asked, sounding concerned. "I wasn't thinking when I asked you to help me. Sorry. I can probably do this myself."

"Oh, no." He moved on to the other foot. "I'm fine."

Dawson was one hundred and eighty degrees the opposite of fine, but he didn't want to deny himself a single second of this sweet torture. So he performed the same ministrations on the second foot as he had on the first. And, even though he knew the nails on its toes would be painted red also, he felt a potent kick of lust upon seeing them.

Afterward, he put her boots over a heat vent on the floor and straightened. "I have a robe you can put on while your clothes are in the dryer."

"Not offering to help me off with those, too?" she asked, arching a brow.

"Would you return the favor?"

She gave him a considering look, but said nothing. Sweeping his arm, he said, "Right this way."

Eve followed him down the hall, past the formal dining room, great room and study. She'd seen some of the rooms earlier today and on a previous visit, but she couldn't help but be curious about the rest of the house. People's homes said a lot about them.

Dawson's told of a fondness for fine things. All of the rooms were large and lushly appointed. She wouldn't call the furnishings fussy or ornate, but they definitely were of the highest quality.

The bedrooms were located on the second floor, up a staircase that curved dramatically around the two-story foyer. Her nerves were humming along on high by the time they reached the master suite.

To one side of the room was a fireplace with its own cozy sitting area. She chose to concentrate on it rather than the king-sized bed. With the touch of a couple buttons, flames shot to life and soft lighting illuminated the room's periphery.

"I think your bedroom is bigger than my entire apartment," Eve remarked as Dawson disappeared into a large, walk-in closet. He emerged a moment later with a sumptuous terry cloth robe in one hand and a fresh change of clothes for himself in the other.

"Here you go," he said, handing her the robe. "You can change in here. The bathroom is right through that door." He backed up a step, looking endearingly flustered when he added, "I'll just…uh…use one of the rooms down the hall."

"Shall I meet you downstairs afterward?"

"Sure. I'll start the cocoa."

"Don't forget the marshmallows," she called as he was closing the door.

Alone, she made fast work of changing her clothes. She was shivering now, gooseflesh puckering her skin. Cold was the culprit rather than pent-up need. Still she wanted to blush when she recalled the wanton way she'd clung to him out in the snow. She hadn't wanted to let go, knowing that once she did he would retreat again to that isolated prison he'd constructed out of guilt and grief. He hadn't withdrawn completely, though his emotions were once again firmly in control.

The robe was too big. No surprise there, but the fact that it smelled like him had her insides curling. Eve turned up the sleeves and cinched the belt as tightly as she could, knotting it just to be on the safe side before gathering up her damp garments and returning downstairs. She found Dawson in the kitchen, standing in front of the six-burner gas stove. He was stirring a pan of milk. He glanced up at her arrival.

She felt suddenly shy. "Hi."

He was dressed in jeans and a chamois-cloth shirt, which he'd left untucked. It was the most casual she'd ever seen him, and by far the most domestic. The wealthy and resourceful Dawson Burke was heating milk to make hot cocoa.

"Hi." His gaze meandered down to her bare feet and she saw him swallow before he looked away. "I should have thought to give you a pair of socks."

"I'll be fine, especially if I can prop my feet in front of a fireplace. There doesn't seem to be any shortage of those in this house."

"No. It has four. All of them gas." He motioned

for her to come closer. "Here. Why don't you take over stirring while I throw your things in the dryer?"

"Are you sure you know how to operate one of those?" she asked dryly.

"I think I can figure it out." Tongue in cheek, he added, "Of course, that's assuming I can remember where the laundry room is."

On a chuckle, she handed over her jeans and socks. "Only the back hem of my sweater was damp and since it's cashmere, I left it to dry in front of the fireplace in your room along with some of the, um, more delicate items."

His Adam's apple bobbed a second time. "Okay."

When he continued to stand rooted in place staring at her, Eve added, "The regular setting on the dryer is fine for those."

Dawson cleared his throat. "Regular setting. Right."

When the cocoa was ready they moved to the sitting room where Eve had sipped tea on her first visit to Dawson's home. After he started the fire, she lowered herself to the rug just in front of the hearth. Making every effort to preserve her modesty, she put her feet as close to the flames as possible.

"Mmm," she said on a sigh. "This feels wonderful." Dawson was still standing. Eve glanced up at him. "Aren't you going to sit down?"

"I was planning on using a chair."

"Why would you do that when there's a perfectly good patch of floor right here?"

She patted said patch of floor. Her smile turned the benign gesture into a dare. Grabbing a couple of throw pillows off the sofa, Dawson joined her. Eve wasn't the only one who refused to back down from a challenge.

"So, how's the cocoa?" he asked.

"Good." She sipped it as if to back up her pronouncement, leaving a fine layer of froth on her upper lip, which she then licked off.

He resisted the urge to groan, but not the urge to touch her. "You've still got a little…" He traced her top lip with the tip of his index finger.

"All gone?" she asked.

"I think so." Still staring at her mouth, he said, "Sorry that I couldn't find any of those little marshmallows to go in it."

"That's all right." Her lips curved. "It was a tall order. You don't strike me as the sort of man who drinks hot chocolate with little marshmallows."

He shook his head. "Not often, no."

"Of course, you didn't strike me as the sort who would tackle me in the snow, either."

"I didn't tackle you. I tried to break your fall," he said.

"Yes, but I only fell because you chased me."

"I only chased you because you threw a snowball at me. Two, in fact," he reminded her. "And I did give you fair warning before you fired a second time."

She took another sip of her hot cocoa and gave

him a considering look. "Okay. I'll give you that. Of course, I'm going to want a rematch. And the next time I can promise you I won't be wearing a pair of high-heeled boots that are far more suited to fashion than they are to function."

"Too bad. I really like those boots." He tortured himself with a glance at her bare feet.

"I loved them." Her lips pursed. "They're probably ruined now."

"I'll buy you another pair," he offered magnanimously.

"That's nice of you, but no need. It was my own fault."

"Agreed," Dawson said and enjoyed watching her scowl. "So, what will you wear for our rematch?"

"A pair of waterproof hikers and my ski bibs and down parka."

"You ski?" he asked, marginally surprised.

"Not really, but I look absolutely amazing in the outfit. Like something out of a magazine." She winked.

Dawson didn't laugh, though she'd obviously intended the words as a joke. "I don't doubt it. I'm beginning to think you'd look amazing in just about anything."

He allowed his gaze to skim over the curves that were partially obscured by thick folds of terrycloth.

"I…I…hmm."

He rather liked knowing that he'd made Eve tongue-tied since the woman had had that effect on him more than once in the past couple of weeks. Though he knew he was playing with fire, he said, "I like what you have on at the moment."

She coughed and recovered enough to joke, "What? This old thing?"

"You know, I never really cared for that robe… until now." He knew he'd never put it on again without thinking of Eve and remembering just how provocative she looked with firelight and curiosity reflected in her eyes.

"I'll take that as a compliment."

He set aside his mug. She followed suit.

"You should," he said.

The space between them diminished fractionally with each breath they took until their faces were mere inches apart. He smelled chocolate, was eager to taste it, but he knew that wasn't the reason he suddenly felt so starved.

"Your hair is still damp," he murmured, reaching up to run his fingers through the loose tumble of curls.

"Dawson." Eve sighed his name and closed her eyes, and just that fast he knew he was doomed. But as he followed her down onto the fire-warmed rug, it felt far more like a resurrection than it did an execution.

He started at her neck, nibbling the spot just below her jaw where he could feel her pulse beating.

Life. It was right there under his lips, inviting him, enticing him.

And so he moved lower, alternately kissing and

nipping his way down to the curve of her shoulder. Her skin was soft and as smooth as satin. When he pushed the robe off her shoulder, it all but glowed in the firelight.

He glanced up to find Eve watching him. Her expression was serious. Her dark eyes were wide and still filled with questions. Dawson wasn't sure he could give her any of the answers she sought. Come right down to it, he had plenty of questions himself.

He started with the most pressing.

"Are you sure?" he whispered.

She paused a moment, an eternity. When she finally nodded, he stood and helped her to her feet. They didn't speak a word as, hands clasped, he led her through the quiet house back upstairs to his bedroom.

CHAPTER ELEVEN

EVE woke to blaring rock music and a man's heavy arm draped possessively over her waist.

She smiled at the ceiling. Life was good.

The electric guitar was gearing up for its solo before Dawson finally stirred. He reached out a hand to swat off the alarm clock that sat on the bedside table. The only problem was that Eve was in the way. His eyes opened as he realized this. His gaze was bleary at first and then clouded with what she recognized as lust.

Oh, yeah. Life was good.

She stroked his scratchy face, reveling in its distinctive masculine feel. "Good morning."

"That remains to be seen."

"Oh?"

He rolled on top of her and murmured something into her hair that she couldn't quite decipher. Not that it really mattered. Words weren't necessary at that moment. Eve understood Dawson's meaning perfectly.

An hour later, they were both out of bed, showered

and dressed. Her clothes had dried. Her leather boots definitely were worse for the wear, but then she'd expected that. Thankfully, Dawson had found a new toothbrush for her in his linen closet, and Eve kept some makeup essentials in her purse. Without the taming effect of a flat iron, her hair had gone curly, but there was no help for that. She brushed it back as best she could and secured it in a ponytail. Satisfied that she looked presentable, Eve ambled downstairs.

It was Saturday, which meant Dawson's house-keeper had the day off. Eve was grateful for that. The last thing she wanted to do was run in to the older woman while wearing the same outfit she'd had on the evening before. She wasn't old-fashioned exactly, but neither was she one to advertise her private life.

She planned to just grab a cup of coffee and be on her way. It might be the weekend, but she had a busy day of shopping ahead of her. She found Dawson in the kitchen, looking every bit as sexy as he had when he'd smiled at her first thing that morning. With minimal effort and very few words, he talked her into staying for breakfast.

He stood in front of the six-burner gas cooktop like a captain standing at the helm of a ship. Glancing at the array of ingredients and utensils spread out on the counter around him, she asked baldly, "Can you actually cook?"

He looked insulted. "I went away to college. I lived in a fraternity house with nine guys."

"So we're having pizza and beer for breakfast?" she asked dryly.

"I can manage an omelet."

"Sorry. I don't know what I was thinking, questioning your culinary abilities. I mean, you did whip up that hot cocoa last night."

"Smart aleck." He motioned toward one of the stools on the opposite side of the granite-topped island. "Go sit down before I rescind the invitation."

"Right." After a two-fingered salute, she did as instructed.

Dawson was surprisingly efficient in the kitchen for a man who was used to having others wait on him. He mastered the eggs, though the toast wound up burned. The coffee was fine, excellent in fact. But Eve suspected that out of all of the appliances in his state-of-the-art kitchen that one was probably the one he operated on his own most frequently.

She ate the eggs, passed on the toast and asked for a second cup of the freshly ground French roast.

Sunshine streamed in through the tall window over the sink, making the room glisten. "I've got to tell you. This is a wonderful room, a chef's dream," she said. "My entire kitchen would fit in your sub-zero refrigerator."

"Can you cook?" he asked.

She couldn't help but laugh as he handed back her earlier insult.

"Yes. I can cook. I went away to college, too." Between student loans and scholarships, she'd managed four years at a state university. "And I get to practice on a regular basis. Unlike you, I can't quite afford to hire out the job during the week, although I do have a pretty close relationship with a Chinese restaurant a block up the street from my apartment. They're the first number programmed into my cell phone and I've got them on speed dial at home, too." She grinned.

"I think I'm insulted."

"Don't be. It goes without saying that after last night you've moved up considerably," she assured him, leaning over to peck his cheek.

Dawson cleared his throat. In the brief amount of time that took, his expression shuttered. Eve knew what he was about to say even before he began speaking. Her sudden clairvoyance, however, did little to blunt the impact.

"About last night, Eve. I hope that you…I mean, I hope that you understand I'm not…I'm not ready for something serious right now," he said. "I may never be."

"Define serious."

"You know what I mean."

"Apparently I don't." She pushed her plate aside and folded her arms over her chest. Beneath them, she swore her heart felt bruised. "Why don't you enlighten me?"

"Eve, I like you. I like you a lot. But I can't…I

can't…" He shoved a hand through his hair and expelled a frustrated breath.

"Actually, you can and you did. Very well, I might add. Twice last night and then again this morning."

She'd hoped for a smile, but he was dead serious when he replied, "I'm not talking about physically."

No. Of course he wasn't. "Which leaves emotionally," she said.

He nodded and she felt her heart start to break. For the first time since they'd made love, she wondered if she'd made a huge mistake. To think just an hour ago she'd awakened with a smile and thought her life grand.

Because far more than her pride was stinging at the moment, she told him, "I don't believe I mentioned expecting to march down a church aisle wearing white anytime soon."

"No. But I need to be sure that you understand where I'm coming from."

She swallowed, raised her chin. "I believe I do. You're saying that our relationship is only temporary."

"*Temporary* is not the word I would have chosen," he said quietly.

"Semantics aside, it's what you mean."

Dawson looked miserable. He looked remorseful. But he didn't contradict her.

Not good enough. The phrase echoed in her head, taunting her. It seemed to be the motto for her life, the tagline that summed it up. She hadn't been good enough for her ex-boyfriend's pedigreed family. And now she wasn't good enough to compete with Dawson's memories of his late wife and the previous life he'd enjoyed as a husband and father.

"I'm sorry, Eve."

Far from being appreciated, the apology only made matters worse for her. Around the lump in her throat she said, "Now I want to be sure that you understand something. I'm not the sort of woman who just hops into bed on a whim."

"I know that—"

"No." She slashed a hand through the air to silence him. "This obviously needs to be said. When I'm with a man, I'm not just marking time until something better comes along."

"I'm not marking time, Eve. I promise you that."

She nodded again. "Also, when I'm in a relationship I'm exclusive and I expect the same in return. Nothing about me is casual, Dawson, if you follow my meaning."

"I do."

"I stayed here with you last night because being with you *meant* something to me." When her eyes filled with tears, she hated herself for the weakness they represented, the futility, but she blinked them away and pressed on. She would have her say now. A good cry could wait until later. "I stayed because *you* mean something to me."

He reached over and stroked her cheek with the

back of his hand. "God, I know that. I'd know that even if you hadn't said as much."

"I'm not expecting a marriage proposal." She'd learned her lesson about such expectations after her long-term relationship with Drew. "But I am expecting you to be honest with me and monogamous for as long…for as long as this lasts."

Her anger and outrage were spent. She wished them back, because insecurity began filling the void.

"You have both," he promised. Then, "And for the record, I'm not the casual sort, either."

She nodded and pushed back the stool so she could stand. Gathering up what remained of her pride, she forced a smile to her lips. "Well. Thank you for breakfast and dinner last night."

"You're leaving right now?"

"I need to be going." *Before I make a bigger fool of myself.*

"Eve." Dawson put a hand on her arm to stop her as she turned away. There really was no need, as his next words rooted her in place. "Since my wife died you're…you're the first woman I've been with. You're the first woman I've even wanted to be with."

She closed her eyes and tried to steel her heart. But how could she not tumble a little further into love with the man after such a soul-baring admission?

"Oh, Dawson." She framed his face in her hands, kissed him tenderly. "Thanks for telling me that."

"You're special to me," he whispered. "Please don't doubt that."

"Okay." Inside her head, a small voice whispered, *Am I special enough to make you let go of the past and start thinking about the future?* She ignored it, stepped back and straightened the hem of her sweater. "I really do need to be going."

"Work?" he inquired.

"Yes."

"It's Saturday."

"I know. There's a great sale at Macy's that started an hour ago. I try to save my clients money whenever I can, but at this point I've probably already missed out on most of the best deals."

Half his mouth lifted in a smile. "Then I suppose I should thank you for staying as long as you have."

She kissed him a second time and, despite the questions and doubts swirling in her head, Eve meant it when she said, "It was my pleasure."

The house seemed especially quiet after Eve left and empty in a way it hadn't felt as long as she'd been in it. Dawson felt empty, too. This emptiness was different than how he'd felt for the past three years and, oddly, less easy to accept. Perhaps because he didn't have to. He had a choice. He wasn't sure he wanted to have a choice.

Restless, he spent the next few hours wandering from room to room. Reminders of Sheila and Isabelle were everywhere in the house. Isabelle had taken her first steps in the great room. She'd earned her first major time-out in there too after she'd taken a crayon to the wallpaper.

Sheila had used their budding Picasso's artwork as justification for redoing the entire room. As he had throughout the house, Dawson had given his late wife free rein. So it was no surprise that everything reflected her appreciation for muted hues and soft fabrics. He'd never had a problem with the décor, but perhaps it was time for a change. He recalled the bold color choices in Eve's loft apartment. Maybe something along those lines.

Especially in the bedroom.

He stood at the side of the bed. Eve had straightened the covers. He picked up one of the pillows and brought it to his face. He swore he could smell her perfume. It haunted him. *She* haunted him. The woman was on his mind, under his skin. That was especially true now that he'd made love to her.

He sank down on the side of the bed with a groan, recalling how soft her skin had felt, how responsive she'd been to his touch, how smug her smile had been when she'd curled up against his side afterward.

Dawson had worried that he would regret making love to her. Not the actual act, but the fulfillment and sense of completion it brought. Surprisingly, he hadn't. He'd meant it when he'd told her that he'd been intimate with no one since the accident. Guilt had always managed to quell any arousal. But he hadn't felt guilty with Eve. In fact, even when he'd wakened with her beside him in the very bed he'd shared with his late wife, he hadn't felt guilty. He'd felt happy and optimistic and eager to not only start the day, but to end it…with Eve.

For the first time in three long years, Dawson had felt truly alive.

That was what had finally stoked his guilt.

Of course, he'd botched things horribly when he'd tried to keep Eve from reading too much into their lovemaking. *Temporary.* Was that really what he wanted it to be?

Even now he could see her happy expression cloud over, though she'd managed to rally admirably. She wasn't the sort to stay down for long. Or more likely she wasn't the sort to let someone see her down.

He'd hurt her. Of all his regrets, that was by far the biggest.

By midafternoon, he couldn't stand being alone in his house any longer. He considered going to his office at Burke Financial. He'd spent more than one Saturday tucked behind his desk browsing through spreadsheets and tracking market trends. But burying himself in work held no appeal today. Another option did. Before he could change his mind, he called for his driver.

"Where to?" Jonas asked as the limo idled in the drive.

"I'm not sure. Know a store where I can get a nice pair of women's boots?"

It was nearly six o'clock and Eve had just come in from shopping when the bell chimed. She expected to find a deliveryman at her door. She shopped online for hard-to-find items, so packages were arriving daily. When she opened the door, however, it was Dawson who stood on the other side. He looked tired and a little lost.

"Hi."

"Hi."

"I wasn't expecting you," she said.

"I know. Sorry. I probably should have called. I won't stay long. I just came to drop this off."

He held out the package that had been tucked under his arm. The rectangular box was wrapped in festive paper, though the print wasn't holiday-themed. The top sported a large and equally festive-looking bow, although at the moment it was slightly crushed.

"What is it?" she asked.

"You'll have to open it to find out."

"It's for me?" She blinked. For a moment she'd thought, hoped, that Dawson had decided to do a little of his Christmas shopping himself. The notion had pleased her, even if it would cut into her commission, but a gift for her? She wasn't sure how she felt about that given the perplexing nature of their relationship.

Dawson nodded. "Your name is on the tag. Unless

I've got the wrong Eve Hawley." He started to pull the package away.

"Oh, no. You've got the right one. And I happen to love surprises." She shook the package and then grinned because she couldn't stop the smile from curving her lips. "Come in," she invited, remembering her manners.

Though she was dying to open it right then and there, she set the gift aside to take Dawson's jacket and hang it up. Then she picked up the box and without another word shredded the paper. She recognized the logo and was laughing even before she lifted the top.

"You bought me boots."

"I said I would. I'm a man of my word," Dawson said.

"I can't believe you remembered the brand and style." She checked the side of the box then and chuckled in amazement. "And my size."

"You're not the only one who's good with details." But then Dawson cleared his throat and admitted, "Actually, I got lucky on the size."

"Well, thank you." She leaned over and kissed him on the cheek.

"You're welcome."

He didn't move, but Eve did. She set the boots aside and gave in to temptation. By the time this kiss ended she was backed up against the closed door with one leg hooked around his hips.

"Well…" he said.

"Uh-huh."

"I…"

"Me, too."

"We're not talking in full sentences," he said on a laugh.

"We are now. So, is Jonas downstairs?"

He glanced at his watch. "For another three minutes. I told him if I didn't return in fifteen he could leave and I'd call him when I needed him to come back."

"Hedging your bets?" she asked on a chuckle.

"I wasn't sure you'd be home or, for that matter, that you'd want to see me."

"So, if you leave right now, you'll still have a ride?"

He nodded. "Well, unless the elevator stops at every floor on the way down. Then Jonas might be gone by the time I reached the curb. Think I should chance it?"

"That elevator is notoriously slow. Just to be on the safe side, I think you should stay." When the corners of her mouth lifted in a smile, his followed suit.

By the time their second kiss ended, both of her legs were wrapped around his waist.

"Loft?" he asked on a labored breath.

"Couch. It's closer."

"Much," he agreed.

Neither one of them wasted time with words after that.

An hour later, as the lamp on the table clicked on thanks to an automatic timer, Eve roused beside him on the couch and stood, covering herself with a chenille throw. She looked uncertain. He knew how she felt.

"I wasn't planning that when I came here today," he said quietly.

"I know." The uncertainty vanished as she smiled. "That's what makes it special."

He smiled in return. "Yeah."

"I suppose I should play the hostess and ask if you'd like something to drink."

He felt chilled now that she wasn't beside him on the couch. "You wouldn't happen to have hot cocoa with little marshmallows? For some reason I have a real craving for that."

"No, sorry. No marshmallows." She huffed out a breath. "No milk for that matter. I haven't made it to the grocery store this week despite my good intentions."

He sat up and reached for his clothes, which were scattered about on the floor with hers. "You're a personal shopper, Eve."

She lifted her shoulders in a shrug. "And the cobbler's children have no shoes."

"Right." He laughed. "I won't ask how you're coming on your own Christmas shopping."

"Good, because I haven't started it. Luckily I don't have much to do."

Dressed, he followed her into the small kitchen, where she uncorked a bottle of wine and poured them each a glass.

"Will you be going back East to spend the holidays with family?" he asked.

"No."

Eve had no reason to make the trip. Her dad was on the road someplace. As for her extended family, even the relatives with whom she had lived as a child had never gone out of their way to make her feel welcomed back into their homes now that she was an adult. Since college she'd spent the holidays with friends or boyfriends. This year, with Carole leaving town to visit a sister in Seattle, Eve had neither.

"What about your father?"

"I got a postcard from him earlier this month. He's playing at a pub in Myrtle Beach through the New Year. He sent me a lovely Laura Ashley–print dress. The pattern is very similar to the wallpaper in your downstairs powder room."

"Floral? You?"

Dawson sounded so incredulous that it made her smile. "Yes. I'm not big on flower prints, but then my father doesn't know me well enough to have figured that out."

"So what will you do?" he asked.

"I could take it back. Whoever he talked into buying it included a gift receipt in the card. More likely, though, I'll donate it to charity." She shrugged. "It's a nice dress, even if it's not my style."

"That's not what I mean, Eve. Where will you go for Christmas?"

"Nowhere. I'll celebrate here. I'm going to put up a tree this week." She glanced toward the living room. "Nothing big, but I want it to be real. I haven't had a real tree in a while. Drew was allergic."

Dawson was frowning. "I guess I just assumed…"

"What? That you were the only one who would be spending Christmas alone?"

"Sorry."

"No, I am. Let's forget that." She raised her glass, inadvertently offering a tantalizing glimpse of flesh beneath the throw. "I saved this Chianti for a special occasion. This is special."

"I think so, too."

Their glasses clinked together before they sipped the wine. Then Dawson said, "Can I talk you into letting me take you out to dinner?"

"Gee, I have some moldy cheddar cheese, half a head of wilted lettuce and some leftover lasagna that could possibly walk out of the refrigerator on its own at this point. If you're offering to take me out to dinner, you won't find me playing hard to get," she assured him on a laugh.

"I'll call my driver. Tell him to give us half an hour."

"We don't need to bother Jonas," she said.

"It's no bother," Dawson objected. "It's what the man is paid to do."

Eve shrugged and reached for her cordless phone. Handing it to him, she said, "Give the poor man the night off then."

"How would I get home?"

"I can take you," she said.

"Oh?" He stepped closer.

"Or not," she added, letting the throw dip low on one shoulder. "I know how you like to make plans, Dawson, but how about we play that one by ear?"

He kissed her bare shoulder. "You know, I'm beginning to like spontaneity."

"I can tell." She sighed before backing up a step and pulling the wrap more securely around her. "I'm starved."

"That's not quite the spontaneity I had in mind."

"I know, but I need to eat. I skipped lunch today. There are a couple of really good restaurants just two blocks over. Or we could go to the market that's on the corner and bring home all of the ingredients for a meal." She smiled. "I could cook for you this time."

"Really?" His lips twitched. "Do you think you can outdo my breakfast, burned toast and all?"

"I'll give it my best shot. My specialty is a pasta dish made with chorizo sausage. It's very good," she promised.

"Sounds like I'll be asking for seconds," he murmured, sipping his wine. His gaze made it clear he wasn't talking about food.

"Asking?" She scoffed. "You'll be begging."

Dawson chuckled. "And what about dessert? Is that included in the meal?"

"Of course. I've got something decadent in mind. I'll

get dressed and we can go." With that she turned and started up the stairs, letting the throw fall as she went.

Dawson stayed the night with Eve and not just because he'd dismissed his driver and it seemed cruel to ask her to drive him home on such a cold night. No. He wanted to remain in her cozy home, in her company. It had nothing to do with sex—as incredible and satisfying as that was—and everything to do with the woman. Eve was like a crackling fire to cold hands, beckoning him to reach out and warm himself.

Parts of him were definitely starting to thaw. The prospect scared the hell out of him because he recognized the feelings that he had for Eve. He'd only felt them for one other woman in his life. And he'd married her.

CHAPTER TWELVE

WHEN Dawson awoke the next morning, the sound-track to *Les Misérables* was playing. He hunted around Eve's bedroom for his shirt, but he couldn't find it. Wearing only his pants, he padded down-stairs. He found her—and his shirt—in the small kitchen. She was wearing the button-down oxford and measuring grounds into the coffeemaker.

"This will be done in a minute," she said over her shoulder.

"No hurry. My shirt looks good on you." He came up behind her, settled his hands on her hips and nuzzled the side of her neck.

"Mmm." Eve issued a throaty sigh. "I live for caf-feine, but I could forgo my morning pot of coffee if I got to wake up to that every day."

He felt her stiffen after she said it and then she turned. "Sorry. I hope that didn't make you uncom-fortable."

"No." It hadn't.

But she was uncomfortable. That was clear when she added, "I don't want you to think we need to go through the whole this-is-temporary discussion again."

"I don't." And he meant it.

The soundtrack came to Fantine's heart-wrenching solo about the life she'd once dreamed of having and the man who'd used and discarded her. It wasn't the ideal song for lightening the mood, but Dawson decided to try to do that by saying, "How about a dance while we wait for our coffee? This time, I'll lead."

"Okay. Show me your moves, John Travolta." She laughed.

Dawson wiped the smile off her face by spinning her out and around.

"Nice," she said once she was back in his arms. "Have you got any others?"

"An entire repertoire."

"Really? Are they all as good as that last one?" She arched one brow.

"Better."

Her dark eyes glittered. "Well, then, by all means. Show me."

None of the moves would have won them any dance competitions, but they were a little fancier than the standard steps.

"Not bad," she said with a dismissive shrug when the song ended. "Maybe I'll let you lead the next time we dance out in public."

"Not bad? What do you think of this?" He levered her backward until her torso was nearly parallel to the kitchen floor. The drama of the move was mitigated by the fact that they'd both begun to laugh.

"I said show me, not show off and put both of our backs out in the process."

Oddly, his back felt perfectly fine. And his shoulders and neck, which were usually tight to the point of going into spasms, were pain-free and almost relaxed.

"Sorry. I couldn't resist doing that," Dawson said as he helped her straighten.

Eve stayed in his arms, her hands flat on his bare chest, her hips flush against his. "What else can't you resist?" she asked.

"I think you know."

"Tell me anyway," she whispered.

"You."

By the time they had both showered and dressed, the morning was spent and the coffeemaker, its pot still full, had shut off. Dawson found Eve sitting on the sofa with one foot perched on the coffee table in front of her. He groaned when he realized what she was doing: painting her toenails.

Red.

"I made a fresh pot of coffee. There's nothing worse than reheated java in my book. The mugs are in the cupboard next to the sink. Help yourself," she told him without sparing him a glance.

When he didn't move, she stopped what she was doing and looked up. "Everything okay?"

"Uh-uh. I've got this thing for red toenails."

Her lips twitched. "On women or is there something you want to tell me?"

"On women in general, but on *you* in particular," he clarified.

"Hmm. Sounds like a fetish."

"I guess you could call it that," he said as he took a seat on the chair opposite the couch.

She pointed the small brush from the polish bottle in his direction. "When we first met, I wouldn't have figured you for the fetish sort."

"Why not?" he asked.

She wrinkled her nose. "Are you kidding? You were much, much too controlling."

"Controlling people can't have fetishes?" he asked, intrigued by her logic.

"Pretty hard to give into your longings when you live by a rigid set of rules."

"You think I'm rigid?"

"No. Not anymore."

"What changed your mind?"

It was a good thing he was sitting down because her answer floored him. "I don't think my mind has changed as much as you've changed. You've loosened up a lot, Dawson."

If that was true, Eve was responsible. And so he told her, "I didn't loosen up, you loosened me. You've been good for me, Eve. A rare and truly unexpected gift."

It was the season for gifts—both getting and giving. But Dawson had long stopped caring about either. Or so he'd thought.

"That's…" Her eyes grew bright. It was a moment before she continued. "That's quite a compliment. I don't know that I deserve it, but thank you."

"You deserve it." He swallowed. "You deserve a hell of a lot more than that."

"So do you, Dawson."

He opened his mouth to disagree, but his standard arguments suddenly seemed worn-out, dated. On the stereo, the persecuted Jean Valjean sang out his name and prisoner number, determined to stop running from the intrepid and intractable Inspector Javert. Eve smiled at him—lovely and oh, so alive. Maybe it was time for Dawson to stop running from his past, too.

Eve drove him home later that afternoon. Halfway to his house, Dawson suddenly changed his mind about their final destination.

"Are you hungry?" he asked.

"Getting there. But I have leftovers from our meal back at my apartment."

"You can't eat that," he told her.

He sounded so resolute that she asked, "Why not?"

"You'll hurt the leftover lasagna's feelings if you do."

"Very funny."

He motioned with his hand. "Take the next exit."

"Where are we going?" she asked.

He compounded the mystery with his cryptic, "You'll see."

Eve followed his directions, turning right on this avenue and left on that one. They wound up in a high-end residential neighborhood where the houses were older and exuded elegance and charm. Almost all of them were decorated for the holidays. In the fading daylight, shimmering bulbs glowed along the eaves and followed the steep peaks of the rooflines.

Dawson told her to stop in front of the one that sported a full-sized manger and Nativity scene in the front yard. She had a good idea where they were even before he told her, "This is where I grew up."

She smiled, and though her throat had grown tight with emotions, she said, "Are you asking me to have Sunday dinner with your family?"

"Yes."

She glanced down at her clothes. "I wish you had said something earlier. For heaven's sake, I'm wearing blue jeans." She shifted in her seat to look in the rearview mirror. "And my hair."

"Is fine. Beautiful," he assured her, reaching out

for her hand when she started to fuss with the curls. "There's no dress code, Eve."

Yes, but outfitted in designer clothes, she would have more confidence. Her gaze cut to the lovely home. It was Tudor-style and even larger than Dawson's. Drew's family had lived in a similarly elegant house. The old vulnerability crept in. "I don't belong here," she whispered.

"Eve?"

She cleared her throat, tried again. "They're not expecting me, Dawson."

"It's a standing invitation," he said.

"For you."

"And for whomever I choose to bring as my guest." He swallowed. "Not that I've ever brought any guests."

And that was exactly why his invitation meant so much to her. Still, she asked, "Are you sure your mother won't mind me tagging along?"

"Not at all. You were at the charity ball. The more the merrier is her motto. Besides, there's always enough food on Sundays to feed a small army." He held out a hand. "So, what do you say, Eve?"

Banishing the last of her doubts, she nodded. "I'd love to."

Dawson's family didn't inspect Eve from a respectable distance this time. They quite literally mobbed her the moment she and Dawson entered the foyer, welcoming him home and welcoming her into their midst with hugs and handshakes, laughter and shouted greetings.

"Christmas came early," Tallulah said as the commotion died down. "I'm so glad you're here and that you brought Eve."

"I am, too," Dawson said. "I am, too."

CHAPTER THIRTEEN

CHRISTMAS Eve was the day after next, but Dawson had not begun to pack for his trip. Usually by this point he had at least worked up a list of summer clothes for Ingrid to wash and press if need be, but he hadn't even done that. He'd been too busy.

With Eve.

They'd spent nearly every evening together since having dinner with his parents. For that matter, they'd also spent nearly every night wrapped in each others arms, warm and worn-out from their lovemaking.

The dawn of a new year was just over a week away, and Dawson felt a sense of anticipation that had been lacking since the accident. And that remained so even with the anniversary of the crash looming like a thundercloud.

That night, he and Eve met Tony and Christine for dinner at the steak restaurant they'd mentioned being keen to try at the auction. The other couple had been surprised when he'd called them earlier in the week to see if they were free. He had the feeling they'd shuffled around their plans to accommodate him. He was glad, grateful.

The four of them chatted amiably through all of the courses. Dawson and Sheila had spent some wonderful evenings in their company. Tonight, the dynamic was different, as was so much of Dawson's life these days. They not only accepted Eve, he could tell they genuinely liked her.

"This was so much fun," Christine said after dinner. "Let's do it again."

"We will," Dawson assured her as he smiled at Eve. "We will."

Eve smiled in return.

Tony and Christine left right after dessert. They had some last-minute shopping to do for their children before heading home to relieve the babysitter. Dawson and Eve stayed for a second cup of coffee.

Eve wished they hadn't, given what happened next. While Dawson retrieved their checked coats, she waited to one side of the lobby. He was on his way to join her when he was stopped by a petite blond woman.

"Dawson!" The beautiful young woman threw her arms around him and then smiled up at him as if he'd hung the moon.

"Natasha, hello." He looked startled. Beyond that, Eve had a hard time gauging his expression.

"Mom and Dad are in the lounge having a drink. We're a little early for our reservation," the woman said.

"How—how are your parents?"

"All things considered, they're well." She sent him a sympathetic smile. "You know how it is. This time of year especially."

"Yes."

"How are you?" she asked.

"I'm fine."

"Dawson, no need for the stiff upper lip around me."

"I'm okay, Nat," he said, nodding. "Better."

She tilted her head to one side. "You've told me that before. But, you know, I almost believe you this time. You look good, happy…almost whole again."

His Adam's apple bobbed. "I'm getting there. And what about you?"

She shrugged, her bright smile wobbled. "I have good days and bad days. More good than bad now. So, I suppose that's progress."

He reached out to squeeze her hand. "I'm glad to hear that, Nat."

"It took a while," she admitted. "And I suppose I should warn you that Mom's not quite there yet."

He nodded solemnly. "I know."

"That's not your concern though, Daw. I know she said some things right after the accident and then at the funeral that made you feel differently, but it never was."

"I wish—"

"Don't," was all she said, giving her head a firm shake. Then her expression brightened. "So, who are you here with? Anyone I know?"

Dawson cleared his throat then and his gaze landed on Eve, who stood just beyond the young woman. He extended a hand to her, in that moment bridging the past and the present. "Eve Hawley, I'd like you to meet Natasha Derringer, Sheila's sister."

Eve had figured out the young woman's identity already. "Hello," she said, accepting Natasha's extended hand for a shake.

"Dawson's a wonderful man. The best." Natasha sent him a warm smile. "It's nice to see him out and looking happy again." The young woman's eyes were bright, her tone sincere.

Since Eve wasn't sure how to respond to such a heartfelt sentiment, she simply smiled.

That ended abruptly when an older couple joined them. While the man gave Dawson a jovial clap on the back, the woman said nothing. Her silence was damning.

"Hello, Clayton, Angela. How are you?" Dawson inquired, looking ill at ease.

"We're doing all right," Clayton bobbed his graying head. "You know how it is."

"Yes."

The older woman made a harrumphing noise and stared off in the opposite direction.

Dawson cleared his throat. "I would like you to

meet a friend of mine. This is Eve Hawley. Eve, this is Angela and Clayton Derringer."

Sheila's parents.

It was an awkward moment, to be sure. Everyone sensed it. Everyone seemed determined to make the best of it...except for Angela. While Clayton greeted Eve with a polite smile, the older woman glared at her with unmistakable contempt and snubbed her attempt to shake hands. Then she turned her venom on Dawson.

"How nice for you, Dawson, that you are able to go on with your life," she spat. "You're out with someone new, acting as if my daughter never existed. As if your own daughter never existed."

"Angela," the older man began at the same time Natasha said, "Mother, please."

"I can assure you, I haven't forgotten Sheila and Isabelle," Dawson said quietly.

He'd been holding Eve's hand. But as he said this, he released it. Connection broken, she thought. Part of her broke, too. Because she knew in that instant that Dawson had returned to the past.

After a round of apologies, none of which was offered by Angela, the Derringers left.

Eve and Dawson left, too. It came as no surprise to her that when they reached her apartment building, Dawson told Jonas to wait for him while he walked Eve to her door.

"You're not staying tonight." It was more statement than question.

He answered anyway as they stood in the elevator and waited for it to reach her floor. "No."

"Are we still on for dinner tomorrow evening?" she made herself ask.

She knew the answer even before he said, "Sorry, but I'm going to have to cancel."

The elevator doors slid open and they stepped out. "Did something come up?"

"I've got some loose ends I need to clear up before the holidays." They reached her apartment door and he cleared his throat. "I also have some packing to do."

"For Cabo?"

He took the key from her hand and slid it into the door's lock. "Yes."

"You're going."

"You knew that I was," he said defensively as they stepped into her apartment.

"I guess I'd hoped you had changed your mind and had decided to spend the holidays with loved ones."

"Christmas isn't a holiday for me, Eve. It's the anniversary of my wife and daughter's deaths. I have nothing to celebrate." The words came out forcefully, angrily.

And he wouldn't have anything to celebrate as long as that was his focus.

"I won't pretend to know how you feel, Dawson. My mother was thoughtful enough to die on a day that didn't hold any other special meaning for me. But I do know how your family feels. They didn't just lose Sheila and Isabelle on that Christmas Eve. For all intents and purposes, they lost you. Just as I lost my dad the day my mother overdosed."

"I'm sorry, Eve."

"I am, too. I'm sorry for my dad that in addition to missing out on so much of my life, he's missed out on so much of his own. He's not a happy man. Are you happy?"

"I don't—"

"Deserve to be happy? Stop playing the pity card. It's gotten old. They died. You lived. Deal with it!" she shouted. "Because in making yourself pay you're making everyone who loves you pay. I'm not just talking about your family now, Dawson."

"No, Eve." He closed his eyes. "You don't love me."

"That's not something you can control."

He stumbled back a step. It was sadly apropos that he was on one side of the threshold and she was on the other. "I'm going, Eve."

"Of course you are." She shook her head sadly. "I have something for you. Something I'd planned to give you on Christmas, but since it doesn't look like I'll be seeing you then, I'll give it to you now."

"You didn't have to buy me anything."

She shrugged. "I wanted to."

She turned to get it, heart all the heavier when Dawson remained in the hallway, ready to make his escape.

"It's not much," she said, handing him the small

package. Working up a smile, she added, "It's one of those it's-the-thought-that-counts type of gifts."

"Thank you."

When he started to peel back the paper, she stopped him. "Don't open it now."

"Okay." He tucked the present into the pocket of his overcoat with a nod. "Speaking of Christmas, my parents usually have dinner around three in the afternoon. I know you'd be welcome there."

The offer made her heart ache all the more. "Thanks, but I don't think so. I'd feel too awkward."

He frowned. "What will you do?"

"I'll celebrate here." And she would. It's what she'd planned before her relationship with Dawson had turned intimate. "I'm going to pick out a tree tomorrow. The apartment will smell like pine needles. I plan to string it with lights and garland and douse it in tinsel."

"And then what?" he asked.

"I'll go to the market and pick up all of the ingredients for a major feast. After eating, I'll put on my pajamas and watch *It's a Wonderful Life.*"

"Eve, you don't have to spend Christmas alone," he began.

"Neither do you. We all have choices, Dawson." She stepped out into the hallway and kissed his cheek. "Merry Christmas."

He was still standing there frowning at her when she closed the door.

* * *

Dawson was in a nasty mood. Damn Eve. She was trying to make him feel guilty, he decided. Yes, that was it. She'd known he would be leaving town for the holidays. He'd never made her any promises.

Nor did she ask for any, his conscience reminded him. Even when they'd lain wrapped in one another's arms sharing their innermost thoughts, she hadn't asked Dawson about the future.

Temporary. That was the adjective she'd applied to their relationship at the very beginning. More accurately, it was what she assumed he intended. He'd let the assumption stand, even though as the days passed it began to feel far more permanent.

We all have choices, Dawson.

He didn't agree. Or at least he hadn't.

On Christmas Eve, he left the office just after one o'clock in the afternoon. The company party was later that day, but he wouldn't be there. He had a flight to catch at six o'clock. Mrs. Stern would see to it that the bonuses were distributed to the employees, just as she had seen to it that the gifts Eve had purchased for clients had been wrapped and delivered.

As for the gifts for his family, Jonas would take those over. Dawson called his mother from his cell phone on the drive home to give her the news. She was very disappointed he wouldn't be there in person, and let him know it. For the first ten minutes of the conversation he wasn't able to get a word in. But then she surprised him by saying, "Well, I hope you and Eve have a good time."

He cleared his throat. "Mom, Eve's not coming with me."

"You're going alone? But I thought… The way you look at her, Dawson. The way she looks at you. It's plain as can be that you're falling in l—"

"No!" He lowered his voice, moderated his tone. "I mean, we hardly know one another."

The excuse rang hollow even to him. The length of their acquaintance had nothing to do with it.

Sure enough, his mother pointed this out. "I fell in love with your father on our first date. He waited 'til we'd been seeing one another six months before he proposed, but he said he'd known I was the one for him the first time he laid eyes on me. That girl is special, Dawson."

"Sheila was special."

"Thinking Eve is too doesn't change that. Sheila was special. But she's gone, son. Don't stay so mired in the past that you let Eve get away."

Because his eyes had begun to sting, he closed them. "Things between the two of us probably aren't going to work out the way you're hoping, Mom."

Tallulah was quiet for a moment. Then she said, "Ask yourself this, Dawson—are they going to work out the way you were hoping?"

After the phone call, he stared out the window at the midafternoon traffic. When he shifted in his seat, something in his pocket bit into his side. He reached into his overcoat and pulled out the gift-wrapped box. Eve's gift. He'd forgotten all about it.

He decided to open it, peeling back the paper and then lifting the lid. She'd told him it was an it's-the-thought-that-counts type of gift. The thought left him staggered.

She'd given him—the man who had boycotted Christmas for the past three years, the man who had refused to acknowledge the past—a small glass ornament in the shape of two embracing angels. He pulled out the note that was tucked inside the box.

For your tree. Hang these angels on the highest branch and when you're feeling sad, take time to remember the love and laughter you shared and to celebrate their lives.

Dawson swallowed. He didn't have a tree. He hadn't put one up in three years. Apparently Eve had thought of that, too. It was being delivered even as the limo pulled up the driveway. Two men were holding the ten-foot-tall fir tree as Ingrid stood wringing her hands.

"I explained to them that you're going out of town and that you certainly would not have ordered a Christmas tree," his housekeeper said.

"It's all right. I'll handle this." And though Dawson was a man of action, a man used to making decisions, he stood rooted in place, staring at the tree for several minutes.

"You going to tell us where you want this, mister?" one of the deliverymen asked. "We've got another half-dozen deliveries to make yet today."

Take it back. That was what he intended to say. It made the most sense. He was leaving. But as his thumb stroked over the delicate angels cupped in the palm of his hand, the words that came out were, "It's time to let go."

To let go not of the memories, he realized, but of the guilt and the anger and all of the other negative emotions that had kept him from not only living but remembering Sheila and Isabelle as anything more than victims.

There was more to the life they had shared than the death that divided them. Eve had known that.

"You want us to let go of this thing?" The man looked incredulous.

"No. Take it in the house. Tell the housekeeper I said to set it up in the great room."

And with that, Dawson headed for the garage.

CHAPTER FOURTEEN

IT had been three years since Dawson had last driven a vehicle of any make or model. His car, a luxury sedan, had been totaled in the accident, but his insurance company had paid to replace it. Dawson had never been behind the new car's wheel. For the most part, it had sat in the garage, though his driver took it out regularly to see to its maintenance.

Parked on the other side of the car was the limousine he'd purchased when he'd hired his driver. It was still warm from his ride home. It was also longer and much larger than the sedan. Buckled in the center of the rear seat, he'd been able to beat back the worst of his fear by using the commute time to read the *Wall Street Journal* or make phone calls.

Now Dawson divided his gaze between the two vehicles. He could summon Jonas. The man probably hadn't yet shed his coat. He could be downstairs and ready to leave in a matter of minutes. But Dawson sucked in a breath and came to a decision.

He hung the angel ornament from the rearview mirror. His hands shook as he buckled his seat belt. It, an air bag and divine intervention had saved his life, or so he'd overheard one of the rescue workers at the scene of the accident say. Dawson prayed for that same intervention now as he shifted out of Park, released the brake and inched the car out of the garage.

He stayed to the side streets, driving slower than the posted speeds and testing the brakes often. The roads were clear, but he didn't want to take any chances. Forty minutes later, his confidence buoyed, he turned onto a busy four-lane, adjusting his speed to keep up with traffic. Finally, he decided to venture onto the highway. He bypassed the entrance ramp twice before he had the courage to turn down it. Thirty…forty…fifty… His heart rate accelerated along with the car. Then he was flipping on the blinker, merging into traffic, on his way to his future, assuming he wasn't too late. On the way, he would have to face his past first.

A mile up ahead was the spot where his life had changed, where Sheila and Isabelle's lives had ended. He hadn't traveled past it since then, even if that meant his driver had to go out of his way. How apropos that Dawson was the one behind the wheel for this trip.

He didn't stop, though he slowed down as he approached the overpass, forcing the cars behind him to brake and shift lanes. A couple of drivers went

around him, one honking and gesturing his irritation. Dawson barely noticed. His attention was on the
side of the road. He waited to be assailed by grief and
guilt and memories. He worried that he wouldn't be
able to continue driving and would have to call Jonas
to come for him and have the car towed back home.

None of that happened.

What had been the scene of horrible carnage three
years earlier, now looked innocuous and surprisingly
nondescript. He felt sad as he drove past it, which
was perfectly understandable under the circum-
stances. But that wasn't the only emotion he experi-
enced. By confronting his fears he also felt free and,
as he depressed the gas pedal, fully in control.

In his head he heard Tallulah asking if things
between him and Eve were going to work out the way
he had been hoping. This time he had an answer.

"If I have anything to say about it they will," he
murmured.

One hour and two stops later, he arrived at Eve's
apartment. Despite his earlier resolve, his knees felt
a little shaky as he waited for her to answer his knock.

She opened the door wearing blue jeans and an
oversized sweatshirt. Her hair was pulled back in a
ponytail. She looked so lovely and so guarded that
his heart took a tumble. What if he was too late?
She'd been hurt before. What if she decided he
wasn't worth a second chance?

"Dawson." She blinked in surprise, though beyond that he had a hard time gauging her reaction. Was she happy to see him? Angry?

"Can I come in?"

Christmas music was playing on her stereo and the scent of popcorn wafted out the door. It was a moment before she stepped back. "Sure."

A small tree was in the far corner of the room, completely dwarfed by the high ceiling. She'd already decorated it with multicolored lights and appeared to be in the process of stringing popcorn and cranberries for a garland.

"Looks like you could use the tree you had delivered to my house," he said.

She closed her eyes and let out a sigh. "I tried to cancel the delivery, but I called too late. Sorry. I placed the order when I thought…well, before."

When she'd thought he was ready to move on. "I also opened the gift you gave me."

She grimaced. "I shouldn't have given you that the other night. I nearly chased you down the hallway afterward and asked for it back. If I've offended you, I'm sorry. It wasn't my intent. I just wanted you to know—"

"That it's okay to be alive."

She nodded.

He walked to the couch and picked up the strand of popcorn and cranberries she'd been making. As he studied it, he said, "I'm never going to feel one hundred percent festive this time of year, Eve."

"No one who knows what you've been through would expect you to be," she said.

"I loved my wife."

"Of course you did. You always will."

"And my daughter." His voice hoarse, he added, "It's hard to imagine how deeply you can love another person until you have a child. All you want to do is protect them and keep them safe." His cheeks were wet.

Eve's heart ached for Dawson. She wanted to go to him and wrap her arms around him. But this was his journey. One he had to make alone.

"Not even the most devoted parent can do that. Some things are outside our control," she said.

He bowed his head and she watched his shoulders shudder with his sorrow, but when he spoke, his words gave her hope. "I've finally started to realize that."

"The accident wasn't your fault."

He exhaled heavily before looking up. "Part of me knows that."

She went to him, brushed away his tears. "The rest of you will accept it in time."

He was nodding as he reached for her hand and brought it to his lips for a kiss. Her heart hammered, but her voice was steady when she said, "I know Jonas is downstairs, but do you have time for a glass of wine before heading to the airport?"

He was still holding her hand, rubbing the palm in that erotic way of his. "Actually, I drove here myself."

"You d-did," she stammered. That was a big step for him, especially on this day of all days.

"It was time." He kissed her hand again.

What else is it time for? she wanted to ask, but she bit back the question. "Since you're driving maybe wine isn't a good idea. I can brew up some coffee. Got time for a cup?"

"Actually, I'm not in a hurry. I'm thinking of taking a later flight."

Something in the way he was watching her had Eve's heart bucking out an extra beat. "You are?"

"I am."

"How much later?" she asked.

"Depends."

Her throat was threatening to close, but she managed to ask, "On what?"

"On your answer to a question."

"A question?"

"More like a proposal," he clarified. At that, her heart sped up, beating so noisily that she wasn't sure she'd heard him correctly.

He was saying, "My travel agent says Cabo can be very romantic. Sandy beaches, gorgeous sunsets."

"Are you asking me to go with you?" Eve asked.

He nodded. "It's a great place to start a new life. A great place to spend a honeymoon."

From his pocket he pulled a small leather box. Her head felt light. "Oh, my God." When he'd said proposal, he'd meant Proposal. With a capital *P*. "You're asking me to marry you."

"I know we haven't known one another long, but I love you, Eve. I didn't think I could feel this way again. I didn't think I wanted to or deserved to."

"What do you think now?"

His cheeks were streaked with tears, but Dawson was smiling at her. He looked happy. He looked whole. He was every inch the authoritative business-man when he said, "I don't think, I know. You're my future, Eve."

Her own tears spilled over even as she kissed his away. She shared his conviction when she replied, "You're my future, too."

MILLS & BOON®
Pure reading pleasure™

SEPTEMBER 2008 HARDBACK TITLES

ROMANCE

Ruthlessly Bedded by the Italian Billionaire *Emma Darcy*	978 0 263 20350 9
Mendez's Mistress *Anne Mather*	978 0 263 20351 6
Rafael's Suitable Bride *Cathy Williams*	978 0 263 20352 3
Desert Prince, Defiant Virgin *Kim Lawrence*	978 0 263 20353 0
Sicilian Husband, Unexpected Baby *Sharon Kendrick*	978 0 263 20354 7
Hired: The Italian's Convenient Mistress *Carol Marinelli*	978 0 263 20355 4
Antonides' Forbidden Wife *Anne McAllister*	978 0 263 20356 1
The Millionaire's Chosen Bride *Susanne James*	978 0 263 20357 8
Wedded in a Whirlwind *Liz Fielding*	978 0 263 20358 5
Blind Date with the Boss *Barbara Hannay*	978 0 263 20359 2
The Tycoon's Christmas Proposal *Jackie Braun*	978 0 263 20360 8
Christmas Wishes, Mistletoe Kisses *Fiona Harper*	978 0 263 20361 5
Rescued by the Magic of Christmas *Melissa McClone*	978 0 263 20362 2
Her Millionaire, His Miracle *Myrna Mackenzie*	978 0 263 20363 9
Italian Doctor, Sleigh-Bell Bride *Sarah Morgan*	978 0 263 20364 6
The Desert Surgeon's Secret Son *Olivia Gates*	978 0 263 20365 3

HISTORICAL

Scandalous Secret, Defiant Bride *Helen Dickson*	978 0 263 20210 6
A Question of Impropriety *Michelle Styles*	978 0 263 20211 3
Conquering Knight, Captive Lady *Anne O'Brien*	978 0 263 20212 0

MEDICAL™

Dr Devereux's Proposal *Margaret McDonagh*	978 0 263 19910 9
Children's Doctor, Meant-to-be Wife *Meredith Webber*	978 0 263 19911 6
Christmas at Willowmere *Abigail Gordon*	978 0 263 19912 3
Dr Romano's Christmas Baby *Amy Andrews*	978 0 263 19913 0

MILLS & BOON
Pure reading pleasure

SEPTEMBER 2008 LARGE PRINT TITLES

ROMANCE

The Markonos Bride *Michelle Reid*	978 0 263 20074 4
The Italian's Passionate Revenge *Lucy Gordon*	978 0 263 20075 1
The Greek Tycoon's Baby Bargain *Sharon Kendrick*	978 0 263 20076 8
Di Cesare's Pregnant Mistress *Chantelle Shaw*	978 0 263 20077 5
His Pregnant Housekeeper *Caroline Anderson*	978 0 263 20078 2
The Italian Playboy's Secret Son *Rebecca Winters*	978 0 263 20079 9
Her Sheikh Boss *Carol Grace*	978 0 263 20080 5
Wanted: White Wedding *Natasha Oakley*	978 0 263 20081 2

HISTORICAL

The Last Rake In London *Nicola Cornick*	978 0 263 20166 6
The Outrageous Lady Felsham *Louise Allen*	978 0 263 20167 3
An Unconventional Miss *Dorothy Elbury*	978 0 263 20168 0

MEDICAL™

The Surgeon's Fatherhood Surprise *Jennifer Taylor*	978 0 263 19974 1
The Italian Surgeon Claims His Bride *Alison Roberts*	978 0 263 19975 8
Desert Doctor, Secret Sheikh *Meredith Webber*	978 0 263 19976 5
A Wedding in Warragurra *Fiona Lowe*	978 0 263 19977 2
The Firefighter and the Single Mum *Laura Iding*	978 0 263 19978 9
The Nurse's Little Miracle *Molly Evans*	978 0 263 19979 6

MILLS & BOON®
Pure reading pleasure™

OCTOBER 2008 HARDBACK TITLES

ROMANCE

The Greek Tycoon's Disobedient Bride *Lynne Graham*	978 0 263 20366 0
The Venetian's Midnight Mistress *Carole Mortimer*	978 0 263 20367 7
Ruthless Tycoon, Innocent Wife *Helen Brooks*	978 0 263 20368 4
The Sheikh's Wayward Wife *Sandra Marton*	978 0 263 20369 1
The Fiorenza Forced Marriage *Melanie Milburne*	978 0 263 20370 7
The Spanish Billionaire's Christmas Bride *Maggie Cox*	978 0 263 20371 4
The Ruthless Italian's Inexperienced Wife *Christina Hollis*	978 0 263 20372 1
Claimed for the Italian's Revenge *Natalie Rivers*	978 0 263 20373 8
The Italian's Christmas Miracle *Lucy Gordon*	978 0 263 20374 5
Cinderella and the Cowboy *Judy Christenberry*	978 0 263 20375 2
His Mistletoe Bride *Cara Colter*	978 0 263 20376 9
Pregnant: Father Wanted *Claire Baxter*	978 0 263 20377 6
Marry-Me Christmas *Shirley Jump*	978 0 263 20378 3
Her Baby's First Christmas *Susan Meier*	978 0 263 20379 0
One Magical Christmas *Carol Marinelli*	978 0 263 20380 6
The GP's Meant-To-Be Bride *Jennifer Taylor*	978 0 263 20381 3

HISTORICAL

Miss Winbolt and the Fortune Hunter *Sylvia Andrew*	978 0 263 20213 7
Captain Fawley's Innocent Bride *Annie Burrows*	978 0 263 20214 4
The Rake's Rebellious Lady *Anne Herries*	978 0 263 20215 1

MEDICAL™

A Mummy for Christmas *Caroline Anderson*	978 0 263 19914 7
A Bride and Child Worth Waiting For *Marion Lennox*	978 0 263 19915 4
The Italian Surgeon's Christmas Miracle *Alison Roberts*	978 0 263 19916 1
Children's Doctor, Christmas Bride *Lucy Clark*	978 0 263 19917 8

MILLS & BOON®
Pure reading pleasure

OCTOBER 2008 LARGE PRINT TITLES

ROMANCE

The Sheikh's Blackmailed Mistress *Penny Jordan*	978 0 263 20082 9
The Millionaire's Inexperienced Love-Slave *Miranda Lee*	978 0 263 20083 6
Bought: The Greek's Innocent Virgin *Sarah Morgan*	978 0 263 20084 3
Bedded at the Billionaire's Convenience *Cathy Williams*	978 0 263 20085 0
The Pregnancy Promise *Barbara McMahon*	978 0 263 20086 7
The Italian's Cinderella Bride *Lucy Gordon*	978 0 263 20087 4
Saying Yes to the Millionaire *Fiona Harper*	978 0 263 20088 1
Her Royal Wedding Wish *Cara Colter*	978 0 263 20089 8

HISTORICAL

Untouched Mistress *Margaret McPhee*	978 0 263 20169 7
A Less Than Perfect Lady *Elizabeth Beacon*	978 0 263 20170 3
Viking Warrior, Unwilling Wife *Michelle Styles*	978 0 263 20171 0

MEDICAL™

The Doctor's Royal Love-Child *Kate Hardy*	978 0 263 19980 2
His Island Bride *Marion Lennox*	978 0 263 19981 9
A Consultant Beyond Compare *Joanna Neil*	978 0 263 19982 6
The Surgeon Boss's Bride *Melanie Milburne*	978 0 263 19983 3
A Wife Worth Waiting For *Maggie Kingsley*	978 0 263 19984 0
Desert Prince, Expectant Mother *Olivia Gates*	978 0 263 19985 7